Port Orford's
YOUNGEST
FISHERMAN

Thank you so much for buying our little Book. Please share it with a young person if you have a chance.

Pete & Kat

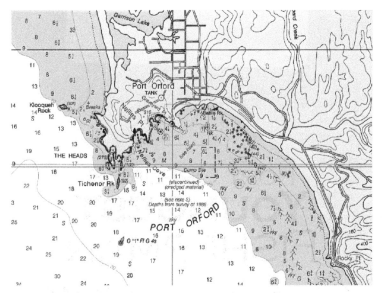

Chart of Port Orford, Orford Reef, and Rocky Point

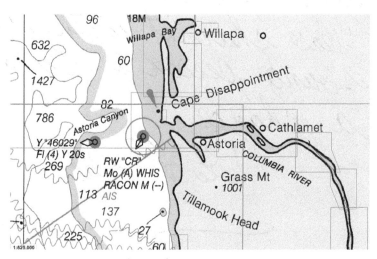

Chart of Astoria Canyon

PORT ORFORD'S
YOUNGEST
FISHERMAN

CAPT. H.J. PETTERSEN

This is a work of fiction. All of the characters, names, incidents, organizations, and dialogue in this novel are either the products of the author's imagination or are used fictitiously.

Archway Publishing books may be ordered through booksellers or by contacting:

Archway Publishing
1663 Liberty Drive
Bloomington, IN 47403
www.archwaypublishing.com
1 (888) 242-5904

Because of the dynamic nature of the Internet, any web addresses or links contained in this book may have changed since publication and may no longer be valid. The views expressed in this work are solely those of the author and do not necessarily reflect the views of the publisher, and the publisher hereby disclaims any responsibility for them.

Cover Graphic by Lance V. Nix

Image credits:
Charts provided courtesy of NOAA and Rose Point Navigation System
Grandpa's fisherman shack – Kevin Kelley
Gear Locker – Dreamstime
Port Orford Dock & Cranes – Lance V. Nix
Boat on Hoist – Alan Haig-Brown

ISBN: 978-1-4808-5046-0 (sc)
ISBN: 978-1-4808-5047-7 (e)

Library of Congress Control Number: 2017950321

Print information available on the last page.

Archway Publishing rev. date: 08/15/2017

CONTENTS

PART 1

PART 2

PART 3

Part Four

A special thanks to my wife and partner in life. If it weren't for her encouragement and support, this book would not have come to be.

My motivation to write this book was to share the dream of adventure with young readers. There is one out there just waiting for each one of you. Thank you for taking time out of your busy lives to read this story.

PART 1

CHAPTER 1

"Grandpa, why would the preacher say Mom and Dad have gone home? You and I both know that's not true. Home is here with you and me, here in Port Orford. I just don't understand why, Grandpa."

"Vell, you know, people tink of heaven as a home. Dey're happy dere. Dey don't have to vorry about no-thing anymore."

"You mean, now you have to worry about me instead of Mom and Dad?"

"Yaw, someting like dat, Cable."

Eight-year-old Cable and his grandpa stepped outside of the community hall and headed for the graveyard. Veda scurried past them and parked herself directly in front of the two Dent men. "Philip, I need to speak with you for a minute right now."

Phil grumbled inside. *I knew this was coming. That old bag Veda has never liked me, and neither has that sloth Burley she shacks up with. It's just too bad dat log truck lost its brakes on da corner on Highway 101.*

Little Cable's folks, Ben and Carol, had just been getting their lives together. After Ben got back from

1

Vietnam, he'd had a lot of problems. Thank God for the VA and the war not hurting him too bad. They'd paid off a few bills, Ben had slowed down his drinking, and Carol had been working part time at the Berquists' general store down at the marina. Things had been coming around for them. Now they were gone.

"Ya, vat is it, Veda?"

"Now, Philip—you realize I'm the boy's grandma, and he should come live with Burley and me now that Carol's gone. The boy needs a woman's care at home, and only we can offer that.

"After all, it's 1980, ya know. And with the courts today, they'll have the boy go to his grandmother, not to someone who's at the tavern all the time and lives in a two-room shack with only an outhouse for a bathroom."

"Now, Veda, you're an old rag, shacked up with that sloth good-for-nothing. As far as drinking, have you checked your garbage can lately? No, the boy stays with me. That's final."

Phil squeezed Cable's hand. "You vant a fight? You got one! Little Cable here stays in Port Orford where he belongs, with his family and friends. So yust forget it now, vill you?"

Phil and Cable pushed past Veda, leaving her gasping for air like a big, fat goldfish in front of the other folks standing outside the community hall. Grandpa was mad. Cable knew he had never liked Veda. He said Veda and Burley were always looking for something for nothing.

Phil held Cable's hand tightly, more for himself than for Cable. *No, they von't be taking dis boy. No one will. He's my son's son, and now it's my job to raise him straight and strong.* "He vill make a fine fisherman," Phil mumbled under his breath, "respected among the fleet, by golly, so help me God."

They walked up the windswept hillside to the cemetery. Heavy, dark clouds from the latest spring storm scudded across the sky. Two fresh holes had been dug side by side in the graveyard. "Grandpa, is that where they will sleep?"

"Yaw, Cable, dey vill be here for you. If you get to missing dem or want to talk to dem, just come up here and have yourself a seat. You yust start talking, and they vill be here listening to you. I tink maybe they vould like dat. Someday you vill put me here next to your folks. That vould be good to keep all of us together, yaw beings we're family and all."

"Yes, that's good. I like that. And it isn't that far from your cabin either."

As they stood next to the graves, the preacher read his part, everyone prayed, and then the caskets were lowered into their holes.

Cable, still holding his grandpa's hand, said, "Goodbye, Mom and Dad."

Grandpa squeezed his hand. Dropping Grandpa's hand, Cable walked up to the two graves and scooped up some fresh dirt in his hand. He put half a handful of dirt in his mother's grave and the rest in his father's. Grandpa had told him that it helped them go back to the earth they loved so much, since that was where we all ended up sooner or later.

Grandpa took Cable's hand again as they walked back down the hill, dotted with trees sculpted by ocean winds, toward Grandpa's fisherman shack. The hill and cemetery overlooked the boatyard in the little coastal town of Port Orford, Oregon.

The marina, dock, and hoists were surrounded and protected by a long, man-made jetty constructed of huge, jagged granite boulders. The dock consisted of a boat storage area and two large, yellow cranes setting atop a thirty-foot-high steel wall. All boats were raised and lowered into the water via one of those cranes, as there was no actual harbor. Boats were stored in the boatyard on homemade, wheeled trailers when they were not being used for fishing. This was a totally unique seaport, the only one like it on the West Coast and home to the Port Orford fishing fleet.

This was where little Cable had been born and raised. He loved it here and wanted to stay with his grandpa. He hoped to someday get a fishing boat of his own and fish with the Port Orford fleet.

Grandpa had taken Cable fishing with him the last two summers, and he looked forward to this coming summer. Cable loved his grandpa, and they made great fishing partners.

As they continued their walk home, Cable heard a voice call out, "Cable, wait." They turned and saw Amy Berquist, the daughter of the folks who owned the general store.

She was older than Cable by a couple of years and was always nice to him, giving him licorice from the candy counter. "I'm sorry about your mom and dad. If you and your grandpa need anything we can help you with, please let us know."

Cable took a deep breath. The fact that Mom and Dad were gone forever was hitting him harder by the minute. Not wanting to cry in front of Amy and Grandpa, he pushed down the lump in his throat and croaked, "Thanks, Amy."

He turned, dropped Grandpa's hand, and took off at a fast walk toward the boats sitting on their trailers in the boatyard. He wanted to hide among them, let all his feelings out, and then get lost climbing on the giant jetty rocks next to the crashing seas. There was peace for him at the jetty. He had gone there many times before.

Now at a full run, he got to Grandpa's boat, the *Tulla*. That meant "Baby" in Norwegian. Cable leaned his head up next to her hull, letting all his bottled-up tears stream down his face, backed with big sobs.

Amy looked at Phil. "Gosh, I'm so sorry. I didn't mean—"

"No now, don't you vorry none, Amy. He's a brave young boy. It had to come sometime. I tink he'll be fine. We need to vait him out. He's safe where he is now, by the boats and yetty rocks."

"I do hope so. Do you think I should check on him?"

"No," Phil said as he put his arm around her shoulders. "Cable, he's yust fine. Give him time. He'll get hungry and come home. His heart is broke, not his stomach."

CHAPTER 2

Reflecting on the day, Amy walked toward home. She and her parents lived above the general store, next to the boatyard. Port Orford had been Amy's home all her life, and she liked having many friends and family close by.

At ten years old, she was a happy girl with her pigtails and blue jeans. Boys weren't even a thought, although she did like Cable. That was because he was always polite, not like most of the other boys. Just because they were raised in a fishing town didn't give them permission to be mean to girls.

"I'm not dirt and won't be treated that way," she told them.

Mom and Dad were opening the store again, now that the funeral for Ben and Carol Dent was over. Amy thought back just a few days ...when she'd heard about the accident. Such a tragedy, to die so suddenly and so young in life. And they would miss seeing young Cable grow into a man. Amy felt tears well up thinking about it. Her mother was setting up the till.

"Mom, I don't know what I would do if I lost you and Dad, like Cable lost his parents."

"You're strong, Amy. You'd work through it. I know you, girl. You have heart and the will to survive, whether Dad and I are here or not."

"Thanks, Mom."

Amy climbed the steps to her bedroom, worried about Cable. She wasn't so sure his stomach would bring him home as Phil thought. Looking out her bedroom window, she could see past the boatyard to the booming waves and heavy spray blowing over the huge granite rocks of the jetty. He was out there among those rocks—Amy just knew it. They were big enough for him to crawl in and hide.

That southeaster spring storm was still building. The waves were getting bigger by the minute, crashing on the jagged rocks, the wind-driven foam and spray flying everywhere.

Coming back downstairs, Amy said, "Mom, Cable's out there, and I want to check on him." She pulled on her tall, rubber fishing boots and long, hooded raincoat. "I think he's down with the boats, and he's hurting bad."

"All right. You be careful. Dad said this storm will come in like a lion."

Amy went out the front door of the store, the wind slapping her in the face. She pulled the raincoat hood down tighter over her head, fighting to get the screen door closed.

She knew the first place to look was the *Tulla*, Cable's grandpa's boat. Amy walked as quickly as she could, leaning into the wind and rain. At the boatyard, she hurried past the front rows of boats.

Finally at the *Tulla*, she crawled up the ladder leaned against the boat's side and called, "Cable, are you there?"

No answer.

She backed down the ladder and continued calling his name as she walked to the back of the last line of boats, the wind stealing her words Then she saw him, standing there staring into the wind, the wild white sea foam flying and waves crashing against the jetty rocks. The noise was deafening. Cable couldn't hear Amy, even if he wanted to. His coat and pants were drenched through to his skin, wet from sea spray and rain. Amy was close now, sure he could hear her voice, but he never turned to answer her, as if he were a million miles away.

She stepped in front of him, yelling over the wind and crashing seas. "Cable! You're soaking wet! You'll catch your death of pneumonia."

He slowly looked up, finally focusing on her deep, warm, brown eyes, returning from wherever he was. "Amy, what did I do wrong? Did I make them mad? Why did they leave," he yelled, "without saying goodbye? I'm their son. Why would they do that?

"You're older than me. You would know. What did I do wrong? Now I'll never be able to hug Mom again. She's gone, Amy. I liked hugging my mom. Why, Amy? Tell me why," he yelled over the storm, tears streaming down his cheeks, red from the cold wind.

Amy held out her arms and said loud enough to hear,

"Come on, you can hug me. You can hug me anytime you feel like a hug."

He collapsed into her arms and started sobbing all over again.

Finally collecting himself, Cable stepped back. "Thanks," he sniffed. "Do you mean it? I could hug you anytime? I don't want to go to that bag Veda for a hug. I don't like her."

Amy started laughing. "Yes. Anytime you need a hug, you come see me, okay?"

They hugged again.

"Let's go home. You need some dry clothes."

Cable nodded. He still felt a hole where his heart was supposed to be, but he didn't feel so alone now.

They walked to the store holding hands, checked in with Amy's mom, and then headed for the fisherman's shack up on the hill. While they walked, they held hands again. Her hand felt warm and comfortable wrapped around his cold hand. As they stepped into the shack, they found Phil sound asleep in his rocker with a newspaper in his lap.

Amy called to him, "Phil, Cable is wet and cold."

"Oh, vat you say? Yes, of course. Cable, you go strip that vet gear off in the da bedroom. Ve vill hang dem on da back porch. I vill get a towel for yous. Thank you, Amy. I fell asleep. Yaw I had no idea."

"He's okay now," she said sternly. "Please try to keep an eye on him."

After Amy left, Cable stripped and dried off, putting on a clean change of clothes.

Grandpa smiled and said, "Vell now, Grandson, are you better?"

"Yes, sir. Better now."

"By golly, Cable. You realize dat Amy girl is like a guardian angel for you? You yust never know. Could be maybe your Mom and Dad had a hand in getting her to vatch over you. Yust never know, Cable."

The next week, they packed up Ben and Carol's house, holding out a dresser and a couple boxes for Cable to go to their shack. Everything else was packed and stored in Grandpa's gear shed.

"Now, Cable, someday vhen you're older, you can come pull all this gear out and go through it. It vill mean more den than now for you. Remember, it vill always be here for you when you're ready to come look through it."

"Thanks, Grandpa. Now can we go work on *Tulla*?"

"Yes, ve can go vork on da *Tulla*. Ve need to get her ready for spring salmon fishing."

The next month went by quickly. Cable was so busy he didn't have much time to worry about his mom and dad being gone. Amy was always close by if he wanted to talk about them, and there was a hug if he needed one.

Chapter 3

Grandpa was down below working on the engine, while Cable was topside scraping old paint off the wheelhouse windows. It was nice to be outside on this bright, beautiful spring day with not a breath of wind for once.

Cable watched an old car pull up next to *Tulla*, followed by a county sheriff's car pulling in behind. Veda heaved herself out of the passenger side of the old clunk car and waddled over to the ladder tied to the side of *Tulla*. Burley sauntered over from the driver's side. The officer got out of his car and nodded to Veda as he joined them.

"Cable," she yelled, "you go tell Philip I need to see him out here on the ground right now." Cable just looked at them, silently, as he thought it over. Veda was getting madder by the second. "Now, Cable," she called, her voice increasing in pitch and volume, "you go fetch him right now."

Cable slowly went around to the cabin door, slid down the inside steps, and sat down next to Grandpa. He was on his knees hunched over the engine, working on a bunch of wires in his hands.

He glanced up at Cable. "Yaw, Grandson. Vat is it?"

Repeating Grandpa's oft-heard words, Cable said, "Bag Veda with Burley and a sheriff, Grandpa. The sheriff has a paper in his hand. Are they going to take me away, Grandpa?"

"Vell, I don't know, Cable. Let's go find out vat this is all about."

"Okay, but I'm staying up here on *Tulla*. I'm not going, Grandpa. I'll run away if they make me go."

"Ve'll see. You scoot out of the way now so I can get through up the steps."

Veda's voice came shrieking through the boat. "Philip, you get down here right this minute. I mean now. We need to talk to you."

Phil stuck his head out of the cabin door, glancing over the rail toward the group of onlookers gathering below. "Pleasure to see you, Veda. You and Burley are looking fit today," he said, leveling a direct slam at them.

The officer climbed the ladder and smiled. Philip came out of the cabin and sat on the hatch cover next to the ladder. The deputy handed him a piece of paper. "Sir, you have now been served, and you must comply with the order."

"Thank you, Officer. Now, vhat am I to comply vith? Can I have a minute to read all this?"

"Yes, but we do need to get on with it. I don't have all day."

"Yes, yes, all right. Fine, fine."

The court order stated that Cable was to be turned over to Veda. *Vell dis is not good. Yust never had a chance to fight it out with the old bag.* Climbing down the ladder, he said, "Vell, Veda, you get to fatten up your and the sloth's velfare checks some more, by golly, now that you're getting the boy in your sorry clutches."

"Philip, he has no business living with a no-good like you," she said loudly enough for all to hear.

Phil smiled politely, turning to the officer. "Do you have a pen, Percy?"

"Yes. Here, Phil."

The crowd was getting bigger, gathering from the boatyard and fish house to see what was going on. The officer could hear some of the men mumbling under their breath as he handed Phil a pen.

Phil signed the paper, stepped over to face Veda, and looked her square in the eye. "Dis is not over, Veda. You got yourself a fight on your hands. By golly, you can count on dat."

The officer gestured with his hands for the crowd to back up. "I know this is a concern to all of you. The paper is a judge's order for the boy to go to the maternal grandmother. Now there should be no concern from any of you on whether this is fair or not. The decision was made by a judge.

"All of you need to go on about your day. This has been settled. It's out of our hands." *These people might be a problem if I don't defuse the situation right away. Loyalty runs deep here in Port Orford.*

Phil stepped over to the growing crowd and stood next to Amy, who was front and center. Phil knew that

Veda and the sloth had no idea about how to take care of Cable.

Veda called, "Cable, you come down here right this instant."

She and Burley waited. And then they waited some more.

"Cable!" she yelled in her best sharp, shrill voice, the fat on her chin vibrating. "This is the last time. I want you down here right this instant."

Cable stuck his head over the gunnel and calmly asked, "Or what?"

"The officer will come and get you."

The officer shook his head. "No, ma'am. I'm here to serve the paper, not chase rug rats on boats up in the air."

Cable and Philip started laughing, along with everyone else.

Veda elbowed Burley. "You do something. Get him down here so we can go."

Burley hollered up at Cable, "You little varmint, you come down here right this instant, or I *will* come up there and tan your hide. You hear me?"

Philip stepped in front of Burley, their noses about six inches apart. With Grandpa a head taller, Burley was staring almost straight up. "You touch dat boy, I'll beat you into next Tuesday. You hear me, you worthless sloth?"

Burley gulped and took two steps back. He could tell the fisherman meant what he said. He would most likely do it, with or without the officer standing right there.

Murmurs were rumbling through the crowd, and tempers were getting shorter.

The officer stepped forward. "Now, everyone, just calm down here one minute. Phil, would you please wait over there?" He pointed toward Amy.

Phil walked over and stood next to Amy again. The officer looked sternly at Burley. "If there is some tanning to do, I'll be doing it, and it won't be that young boy up there."

Burley took two more steps backwards. He was more than halfway back to their old jalopy car, thinking he might not make it out of there without running for it.

The officer stepped over to the ladder, climbed up to the bulwarks and poked his head over the rail. After removing his hat, he could see Cable just inside the cabin door. The officer asked calmly, "Now, son, you don't want to get your grandpa in trouble, do you?"

Cable thought how much the officer sounded like his dad. He answered quietly, with a respectful tone, "No, sir, but I don't want to go with them. They're mean. I belong with my grandpa."

"I understand that, but they have a paper that says you have to go with them. The judge has decided that for you. If they're mean or hurt you in any way, you tell your grandpa right away. He'll know what to do."

"All right. I don't want him in trouble because of me."

The officer climbed down and stood at the foot of the ladder. Next came Cable, slowly climbing down the ladder to stand by the officer.

"He will go with you. Now let me be clear, so there is no misunderstanding. If anyone lays a hand on this boy, they must answer to me personally. Am I clear?" the officer said, staring at Veda with a hard look. He glanced at Burley, who quickly looked away.

Veda's plump cheeks wiggled as she smiled. "Thank you, officer."

She took Cable's arm forcefully, trying to steer him to the waiting car. Cable jerked his arm away and ran over to Grandpa, giving him a big hug. Looking at Amy, Cable smiled and said, "Can I have one of those hugs you promised me? I think I need one."

"Sure," she said. He wrapped his arms around her and put the side of his head on her. Her chin was above his head as she wrapped her arms around his shoulders. They stood there for a quiet moment.

Veda started chattering again. "All right. All right. Enough. Let's go. Get in the back of the car, Cable."

Burley took Cable's arm to help him along. Cable jerked away with a defiant stare and walked to the car alone.

Veda and Burley finally got in the car and started driving away. Little Cable was on his knees on the seat, looking out the back window, staring at Grandpa and Amy in the afternoon sun of the boatyard.

The officer approached Phil and Amy. "Phil, I'm sorry about Ben and Carol. My apologies for missing the service. You be sure and let me know if they touch the boy."

Phil nodded yes.

"You might like to know why he gave up so easy. The truth is, he didn't want to get you into trouble. Now that's loyalty. He's a good boy, Phil, like his dad."

"Thanks, Percy. It makes me proud to hear that coming from you."

***

Driving up Highway 101 to Coos Bay, Veda was cackling and complaining about Grandpa. Then she was complaining about how much work it was to get the paperwork done to bring Cable home with them, not to mention the time needed to track down a cop to serve the papers on that worthless Philip Dent.

"Carol never should've married Ben Dent in the first place," she rattled on.

That just firmed up what Cable had always known—Veda didn't like his dad.

Cable sat quietly in the backseat waiting for his chance to escape. *This will work*, he thought as they pulled into the Bandon Shell station and restaurant.

Burley wanted a quick beer to settle his nerves after all the recent stress, and Veda wanted to use the ladies' room. "Now, Cable, you are to stay here. Don't get out of the car. We're only going in for a minute."

"Okay." Cable kept his eyes on the floor, not looking up. The doors slammed shut, telling him both were gone. When they drove into the parking lot, he had seen Mitchell O'Leary's fish truck at the gas pumps, pointing in the direction Cable had just come from.

He slipped out of the car and headed straight for the back of Mitchell's flatbed truck. There were fish boxes in the back, covered by a heavy green tarp. Cable hopped up on the back of the truck and lay down beside the boxes, pulling the tarp over himself.

He could hear Mr. O'Leary put the gas nozzle back into the gas pump, whistling a tune and then walking to the back of the truck. Mr. O'Leary pulled up the tarp, gave Cable a big wink and a smile, fiddled with putting the tarp down again, and continued whistling his happy tune.

As Mr. O'Leary went in to pay for the gas, Cable started getting nervous. What if Burley and Veda saw something or started back to the car? But then he could hear Mr. O'Leary's whistling as he got in the truck and drove out of the gas station, toward Port Orford. Not more than ten minutes later, he pulled over at a turnout on the highway. Walking to the back of the truck, he lifted the tarp and smiled. "You might want to ride up front. It's much more comfortable, Cable." Mitchell had known little Cable since he was a baby, and he knew there must be a good reason for Cable hiding in the back of his truck.

Cable hopped down, smiling. "Thank you, Mr. O'Leary!" Once he climbed into the passenger side of the truck, he explained what had happened.

"So the old bag tried to kidnap you?" Mitchel asked with a laugh.

"Yeah, I'm just not going there. I want to be with my grandpa, and with Mom and Dad close by on the hill, and all our friends in Port Orford."

Mitchell nodded. "I sort of thought that, with you keeping my fish boxes company back there." He went back to whistling his tune.

As they pulled into the boatyard by Mitchell's fish

house, Cable slipped out of the truck and went straight over to Grandpa's gear locker. He was figuring to lay low for a while, sure they wouldn't look there. He closed the door quietly behind him and started to sit down. The door opened just enough for someone to slip inside.

"Hey, hi. How did you know I was here?"

Amy was glad to see him back so soon. "I saw you ride in with Mitchell and then sneak over here. So how did you give'em the slip?"

"We pulled in at the Shell in Bandon. Burley wanted a beer, and Veda needed the can. That gave me a chance to slip out of the car and into the back of Mitchell's truck. He saw me but let me ride anyway."

"What're you going to do, Cable? You know they're going to come back for you."

"That's why I'm here. They'll check the shack and *Tulla*. I should be okay here. I don't think they know about the gear shed, and Grandpa won't tell them."

"Okay ... You spending the night here?"

"Maybe. Not sure. When I was listening to them talk in the car, all they wanted me for was the folks' pension money for childcare. Grandpa said he didn't need it; he would rather have me. I think he should get it. He has it coming."

"Do you want some supper?"

"Could you, please?"

Amy's mother caught her trying to get out of the house with a plate of food. Amy couldn't help but tell her everything. Amy's mom made her go tell Phil after she dropped off the plate of food to Cable.

Grandpa showed up shortly after, and Cable filled him in.

"Vell, you know, you might yust be right there. If dey get the money, den dey might leave us alone," said Phil with a big smile.

"But that's your money, Grandpa."

"We von't vorry about dat for now. If dey come back, we must give Social Security a call, do you tink?"

They all had a good laugh about that.

CHAPTER 4

Veda never came looking for Cable, and Grandpa didn't report her to Social Security. He just wanted to keep her out of their lives.

School was a problem. The *Tulla* needed to start the fishing season first part of May, and there were still six weeks of school to be finished. The school wouldn't budge, so while Grandpa took the *Tulla* out, Cable had to stay on the beach some place, four nights a week.

Philip approached Amy's folks, Sam and Adaline Berquist. They said yes to keeping Cable, but there were strict rules. Cable was good with all the rules. In fact, he came in early to help Amy stock shelves in the store, and he washed dishes after supper. He and Amy would sit at the kitchen table in the evening to do homework.

Cable liked doing homework with Amy so much that he picked up extra work at school so he could stay busy at the table and not bother Amy until she had her schoolwork finished.

When he had a problem with his homework, Amy would stop and help him. She was two years older and, in Cable's opinion, a whole lot smarter. He liked having such a helpful friend, and they enjoyed each other's company very much.

Grandpa was home Friday night through Monday mornings. Spring fishing was only average, he had told Cable. Grandpa went to the tavern in the evenings and was late coming home sometimes. Then he would stumble through the door and crash on his bed. That's when the snoring would begin and last for most of the night.

Cable would get up and go down to the *Tulla* to sleep. It was quieter there, and he had his own bunk with a sleeping bag.

Grandpa never worried about him. He knew where Cable was.

When June finally came, Cable could fish full-time for the rest of the summer. The school even let him out two weeks early because he had all his work done.

He would miss staying with the Berquists, but most of all, he would miss spending time with Amy. Fishing was more important though, as that's how he and Grandpa made their living. Grandpa was teaching Cable as much as he could about running the boat and navigation, even in the fog, and about all types of fishing gear, especially when and where to use each kind.

There was so much to learn, and Grandpa would test him from time to time. They were great fishing partners, and life was good for the two of them.

In the middle of the season, with the entire fishing fleet active, the Feds had a closure on Coho salmon, so Grandpa and Cable changed gear and rigged up for tuna trolling.

Cable was thirteen years old now, soon to be fourteen, and Grandpa had turned eighty early that spring. Grandpa mostly drove the boat and had Cable do all the work, including all the thinking. He hadn't told Cable, but this might be his last season, with his arthritis and all. Then, hopefully, he could make it living at the fisherman's shack until Cable was a full-grown man. He wanted to go to the veteran's home to live after that. It would be easier on him.

Grandpa thought Cable had grown a foot in the last year. Before, he was a head shorter than Amy, and now he was almost six feet tall and a full head taller than she was. Amy would be sixteen and driving come Christmas time and was becoming quite a young woman, with her long, brunette hair in a silky ponytail, too old now for double braids. She still had beautiful, warm brown eyes, "and a nice trim shape too," Grandpa would say respectfully.

Amy and Cable were the best of friends. Cable knew he was younger and thought maybe someday an older guy would come along and sweep her off her feet. He was thinking that was the way it was supposed to work.

All the gear had been re-rigged for tuna and provisions put on board. Cable was already on board, excited to be out fishing again. Grandpa climbed aboard, making his way over to the steering seat in the cabin. The *Tulla* was ready to go in the water, and Jan Kayden was operating the crane—Grandpa called it a Jinn pole—as it lowered *Tulla* into the water.

Cable stood by the straps, ready to unhook them, waiting to hear the engine start. There was no sound, not even the starter cranking the little Perkins Diesel engine.

He jumped into the cabin and found Grandpa slumped over the wooden steering wheel. He shook Grandpa, gently at first and then with more urgency. "Grandpa, Grandpa! Wake up! What's wrong?"

Cable jumped out on deck, hollering up to Jan. "Something's wrong with Grandpa. You need to pick us up!"

As the boat came up, putting the deck even with the top of the dock, Cable hollered, "Jan, please call an ambulance! I think Grandpa's had a heart attack or something."

Cable dove back into the cabin. Still no movement from Grandpa.

"Help is on the way," Jan hollered over.

Cable was a big, strong boy now, and he pulled Grandpa out of the cabin, laying him on the hatch cover.

Jan hopped on board, helping Cable bring him to the rail, where Mitchell and one of his workers were waiting. Between the four of them, they got Phil's limp body over the rail and quickly carried him across the boatyard, laying him on the ground near the fish station. Cable took off his coat and gently put it under his grandpa's head, noticing how pale and tired he looked. And Cable realized how old he looked. There was still no sound from him, and his breathing was shallow. The ambulance siren could be heard coming from town.

Amy came running down the hill with her store apron still on. Word had spread quickly that something had happened to Phil. When they were loading him in the ambulance, Amy said, "Cable, you go with him. Jan can take care of *Tulla*, and Mom and I will catch up with you at the hospital. Now go!"

Cable jumped into the back of the ambulance as they slammed the doors behind him. With lights and sirens going, they raced out of the boatyard.

***

Cable was waiting next to the emergency room door when Amy and her mom found him, a scared look on his face. "What have they told you?" Amy asked.

"They said he had a stroke and that he might lose his right side. I don't know what we'll do. He is all I have, but for you and your folks … The good news is, he will live."

Amy put her arm around his waist. He was too tall for her to hold him like she did a few years back.

They sat down and waited for what seemed like an eternity. The doctor finally came in and spoke to them. "He'll be fine, but he did lose the use of his right side. We need to keep an eye on him for a week or so. Is your Grandpa a veteran?"

"Yes, sir. US Navy. He joined when he jumped ship in Seattle in 1916. There was a war on and the Navy was glad to have him. We have his discharge papers at home."

"Good. We might get the VA to help you out with his costs and care. We'll check into it for you. You can go in to see him now."

"Thank you, doctor. I'll make sure you get his papers from the Navy."

The three of them filed in to Grandpa's room, Cable

first. He took Grandpa's big rough hand. "That was quite a scare for all of us."

Grandpa smiled weakly. "Vell now, Grandson, I was tinking of going on my pension next year anyway."

"Grandpa, what about *Tulla*? Who will finish the fishing season? We need the money to live."

Grandpa looked at Cable and smiled, "Now tink about it, Grandson... Who might there be? I tink you vould outwork anyone we put on *Tulla*. Dis vill be your time, Cable. You take her out. She is all iced, fueled, grubbed up, and ready to go make dat tuna trip."

"No, I'm not ready yet, Grandpa."

"Ve think you are. Yaw you just don't know it. Now you go show yourself you can do dis. You call Yohn Dill on da VHF when you get out fifty miles or so. You tell him vhat happened; he vill help you out. I know you'll listen to him. Yust stay close. Yohn won't do you wrong. By golly, I helped him. He is a fine friend. I know he'll help you."

"I'm not sure about this. You trust me with *Tulla*?"

"Yaw, I do. Who do you tink has been running tings for the last two years? I yust been riding along vith you both."

Cable's mind was running full tilt. This was so much to take on. *Grandpa's right. I've been doing most everything the last two years. But this is still a huge responsibility.* Grandpa visited with the ladies while Cable thought it all over.

Grandpa spoke up with a smile, pushing Cable along. "Vhy don't you go ahead and go now? Then maybe I can get some rest. In an hour, you can be running for the tuna grounds. So you scoot now. Remember, ten days on ice is all you get. You don't vant no spoiled fish now."

Cable's heart raced as the possibilities ran through his mind. *I can do this. I can fix almost anything. I'm a good fisherman, and we need the money.* "All right, Grandpa. I'll do it. You take care. I'll see you when I get back. Maybe Amy and Mrs. Berquist can bring you home when the doctors kick you out of here."

"Yaw, dat sounds good. I vant to sleep now, so get going vould you?"

Cable sat in the back of Mrs. Berquist's car, his mind still going a hundred miles an hour. *Once I get going, it'll be easy. Tuna are the most fun fish to catch. I need to make this work. I need to make this work for Grandpa and me.*

PART 2

CHAPTER 5

After pulling into the store's parking lot, they got out of the Berquist's car.

"Thank you both for your help," Cable said in a half-dazed tone, his mind going over every detail of the upcoming trip. "Guess I'll be back in a week or so, maybe two."

Amy stepped toward Cable, "Wait, I'll walk down to the boat with you."

Amy took Cable's hand as Mrs. Berquist watched them walk away.

"Cable, when you pull into another town to sell your fish, you call me. I don't care what time it is. I just care about you and want to know if you're safe. You hear me? That ocean is a big place, and a lot can happen to a person all alone out there."

"Amy, I'll find John Dill and fish next to him. Grandpa taught me well. He's right, you know. I must show myself that I can do it. And this has to be done to make the money needed to take care of Grandpa, *Tulla*, and me."

"Yes, I knew you were going to say that, Cable. Just don't take any chances, for me, please. There is only one of you, and I want to keep you around. Darn, I wish I were going with you. You're so young."

Cable got Jan to put him and *Tulla* in the water. Starting her little engine and stowing the lifting straps, Cable gave a smile and then a big wave to Amy and Jan as he pulled away.

Amy was still skeptical. "Jan, I don't know. He's so young, and the ocean is so big."

"He'll do fine, Amy. You'll see. He was taught by one of the best in our small fleet here. When you do hear from him, be sure and keep us informed. I like to keep track of all of them, especially our youngest Port Orford fisherman."

She smiled and nodded her head, turning back for the store.

***

Tulla headed out around the end of the jetty, clearing the coast guard sea buoy. Cable set the autopilot due west as the jetty, sea buoy, and Port Orford shrank in the distance.

The little boat ran all night with the big wood fishing poles mounted on the side of her in the down position. The stabilizers would have slowed him down, and he didn't mind the extra rocking and rolling *Tulla* did without them.

The weather was good; the sea swells were four feet out of the west and the wind less than five knots. The autopilot was doing a good job steering them in a westerly direction. He was hoping to find John on his boat, the

Orford Reef, somewhere fifty miles off the coast, along with the rest of the fleet.

There was work to do getting all the jigs set up back aft, in the cockpit. Cable planned to have the gear in the water at daylight after running all night. He would find 62° Fahrenheit blue water, just the right temperature for tuna. Tuna liked the warm water, but they would dart over into the colder green water to find more feed and then come back into the warm water.

"Usually, yust the big ones do dat," Grandpa would say, "because dey have more fat, like me." Then he would give his big belly laugh.

Grandpa liked fishing along the coast, on the green waterline. Cable would rather chase the schools farther off shore and stay with them, watching for signs from the birds and drift that showed him where the fish were.

The ocean is calm tonight, Cable thought, sitting in the helm chair and taking short catnaps. He said a little prayer for his grandpa, thanking him for sticking around even if he couldn't fish anymore. He was safe, and the right people were keeping an eye on him.

Grandpa had nothing to worry about anymore. Cable would take care of things. He knew this to be true, because Grandpa had given him all the tools he needed. Cable was born to be a Port Orford fisherman.

And Amy was always on Cable's mind. She was beautiful, with long, soft, silky, brown hair. And a forever smile wrapped smoothly around her deep, sparkling, brown eyes, just above her perfectly shaped nose and those wonderful lips.

Yes, those lips! Cable sat there in the helm chair, staring out the bridge windows into the complete darkness, sprinkled with only a few horizon stars.

Back to those lips. Early this spring, Cable and Amy had gone for a walk along the long, sandy beach south of Amy's folks' store. That was where she'd decided it was time they should kiss for the first time.

"So we could see if there was anything to it," she said.

Cable wasn't so sure about the whole thing. The day was getting late into the evening, and darkness wrapped its arms around them as they walked along the waterline. Amy was smooth about it, saying, "Let's go up and sit on a log. I'm getting cold. I want you to put your arm around me, Cable."

"Okay … but would you rather walk home a little faster to warm up, and we would be home in no time? It's always warm there."

"No, that wasn't what I was thinking. I think it would be nice to have you put your arm around me. We could watch the evening stars come out over the ocean. Then we could just sit and talk about whatever comes up. How does that sound?"

"Well, okay, I guess. I just don't want to have you in late and make your folks worry."

They sat on a large log deposited by a winter storm on the drift line of the beach. Cable felt uncomfortable putting his arm around her shoulders. Amy reached up, took his hand, and tugged on it lightly, to pull him closer.

Cable smiled in the dusk of the evening.

Amy smiled back. "It feels good to be close, doesn't it?"

"Yes, it does. We've been holding hands since I was eight years old. I have always felt close to you, Amy."

"I know, but this is different, don't you think?"

"Yeah ... I think this is the closest we've ever been."

"Would you like to be just a little closer?" Amy asked.

Cable stalled out, his mind drawing a blank. *Now how would we do that?*

Amy felt him backing up a bit, a confused look on his face. She put her hand over his and gently tugged. Without saying a word, she leaned forward and kissed him on the lips. Cable didn't move. He had known this was coming for quite a while. He just hadn't realized she wanted a kiss now.

The moment seemed to last for forever. He felt the heat of their kiss, like "electricity of the connection." That was the only way he could explain the feeling to her on the way back to the store. Amy said she'd liked it too; there was definitely a connection there. Cable asked if she was sure she wanted to kiss with a younger kid. Didn't she want to kiss an older guy?

Not an older guy, and a younger guy was perfect, as long as he was her Cable, she had said. He was the one she wanted to share her first kiss with; that was plain and simple for her.

They'd never talked about their kiss after that evening on the beach. She had kissed him on the cheek as he'd gone to get on *Tulla* for this trip today. Cable knew he would never forget that small moment of magic he'd shared with Amy as long as he lived.

As dawn arrived, the little engine purred along at a

good six knots, which was perfect for tuna speed. Still tired, Cable stretched as he got out of the seat, working the stiffness out of his body from sitting all night. *This will be a beautiful, calm day for fishing. Thank you all who had a hand in bringing me here.*

Cable reflected on how much he loved being out here, with or without someone else on the boat. When he and Grandpa fished, Grandpa taught him to put the boat in a big, broad circle first thing every morning. Sometimes the tuna would hang around the boat at night feeding. He began throwing the jigs he had prepared during the evening into the water.

The fish started hitting immediately. *Bing, bang, bang,* three fish were on the jigs, pulling the hand lines straight back from the trolling poles. Then six more lines were loaded up with fish on them. Cable hauled fish and gear as fast as he could, starting a slow turn to the right to pick up the school and hang onto them. As he landed the fish, their tails rattled like machine guns against the deck. It was music to Cable's young ears. With all the noise and the acrid smell of tuna blood in his nostrils, he was reminded of Grandpa when he would say, "This is Valhalla" (heaven).

By 8:00 a.m., the bite was over, and the deck and bins were full of fish. Cable jumped in the hole when the fish had cooled down a bit and stacked them, adding ice between each layer. Forty-seven fish! Grandpa would be proud. Using the loran, he took a fix on his current position, noting on his chart where the fish had originally started to bite. He drew an imaginary line between the two points and began running back and forth on that line. The tuna were still there, and he got ten to twenty fish an hour. Once they climbed on the feather jigs, he immediately put the boat into a circle and tried to keep the tuna school with him.

Tonight, I'll give John Dill a call, like Grandpa said. The sun finally set, and Cable shut the motor off and iced down the last of the fish. He didn't count them this time. Grandpa said it was bad luck to do that before you sold your fish. *And we need all the luck we can get, old girl.*

Cable laughed to himself at what Grandpa would say. *Tulla's* a boat with a Norwegian name, but she was built by a Finlander. He would bet some Finlander was rolling over in his grave knowing *Tulla* was Norwegian for "Baby." Grandpa had a big sense of humor about almost everything, always laughing and making jokes.

After fixing some dinner, Cable called for John Dill on the VHF radio, "*Orford Reef, Tulla*, over."

No answer.

He listened to the other fishing boats, where they were and their numbers. It was a big ocean, and they needed to share information with one another.

Cable was so new and shy about using the radio that he just listened after calling for John, not giving his name or location. He went to bed about ten that night, turning on the mast light and drifting during the night, planning to be up again at 4:00 a.m.

Day two was the same routine—gear in the water, big circle with the boat, *bang, bang*, small clatter. And then the fish quit biting and everything went quiet. No birds, no feed. He took a new fix on his chart to compare his location to where he had stopped last night.

With that information, he decided to work toward the main fleet farther out and up the coast. *Tulla* was already more than fifty nautical miles out, and Cable was quite comfortable being with her in the middle of the ocean. He knew the boat, its engine, the navigation electronics, and especially all the fishing gear.

He had been taught well. That was the gift Grandpa had given him. He remembered starting when he was six years old. He was thirteen now, fourteen in a few days. *That's eight seasons with Grandpa. I sure miss him.*

I'll call Amy as soon as I get in to see how he's doing.

I think Grandpa was right about another thing. Amy has been a guardian angel for me. Even now, she keeps an eye on me, gives me a hug now and then, not to mention the one kiss. She even holds my hand like when I was eight. It does feel good, with her hand so soft and warm, especially when she squeezes mine. My hands are so hard from always fishing and working on the gear. I don't know how to thank her.

Cable continued working his way north to catch up with the fleet. His last fix had shown him to be about fifty nautical miles due west of Bandon on the Coquille River and twenty-five nautical miles north of Orford Reef. He was running with the gear out, and by late afternoon, the fish started hitting hard again. Every time he put the gear back in the water, more tuna hit the lines, and they didn't stop until sunset. *Darn, I think I found them!* Cable couldn't believe he had done it.

Running out of room on deck, he threw open the small hatch cover and put the coolest ones in the fish hold. He covered the remaining hot fish on deck with gunnysacks, and wet them down when he got a break. At dusk, as he pulled the last of the gear in, fish were flopping everywhere on deck.

He called for John on the radio again, and finally, he was in range to answer. Cable told him about Grandpa and that he had been told to call John. They talked fish numbers. John only had half of what Cable had caught today, and he was a couple of hours north of him.

John said, "You stay right there. We'll run to you tonight. That's good fishing, Cable."

Cable finished icing down his fish, made dinner, and went to bed. He got up in the middle of the night to look around and counted six mast lights around him. The Orford fleet was here, and it felt good to see them. "We need to stick together," Grandpa would always say.

Cable got up early and had the boat running as dawn was cracking. The gear went into the water, and he did the big, slow circle, not wanting to give up his school of fish. *Boom, boom, bang*; the lines loaded up. It would be a long day! By 10:00 a.m., he had a full deck load and stopped just long enough to throw them in the fish hold and ice them down.

He didn't even stop to eat; too much fast action going on. Cable was stoked and wanted more. He continued to pull and reset his lines as hard and fast as he could. The other boats, out of respect, stayed clear of Cable's circle.

If they were to come in too close, they could pick up the school of fish Cable had following him.

Just like yesterday, the bite slowed at noon. That gave him time to ice down the fish and get something to eat.

The radio cracked and John called, laughing, "Cable, you do any good?"

"Yes, sir! About the same as yesterday. Think I'll ease my way to the southwest. I drifted a lot last night."

"Okay, sounds good. Thanks for the tip. We doubled what we had yesterday."

"That's great, John. Keep in touch."

John looked over to his deckhand, who was also his youngest son. "Do you realize he will turn fourteen this month? Old Phil taught him good. He will outfish us all. You keep an eye on him, and you just might learn something."

Trolling at six knots an hour, before long Cable was over the horizon from the rest of the boats. He found a bunch of tuna birds working an area, diving in and catching fish. He could hear Grandpa telling him, "You stay on the outside edge; yust don't disturb them. Den you can catch fish all day long."

He went to work, pulling about twenty fish an hour and, by afternoon, had yet another deck load. Time to ice them down.

"Ya, John, you might want to come my way," he called on the radio.

When Cable was six, Grandpa and Dad had spent the winter rebuilding *Tulla*. They had taken off the aft cabin, decked her over with a new hatch, and slid the engine and fuel tanks forward four feet. That had made her a little bow heavy but doubled her packing ability. And Cable was putting it all to good use.

There were a lot of times Grandpa would deck load her, and it was Cable's hope to do this on his first time out—fill the hold completely, and then fill the deck. One more big day, and he would have that. Then he would head back to Port Orford to check on Grandpa and sell his fish.

The afternoon start was slower than the other days. John decided to move north, but Cable knew that was not a natural track for the fish. He fretted long and hard. *It could be we're only on the edge of the fish.*

"Think I'll fish to the northwest, John. I'm going out to about seventy-five miles off shore."

"Well, okay. Keep me posted, would ya?"

"Oh, you bet ya, John."

The hot afternoon sun beat down on Cable as he stood in the stern cockpit, leaned up against the cockpit coaming. There was not a breath of wind. Only the quiet purr of the little Perkins diesel kept him company as he waited for the next strike.

Pow!

Suddenly every jig had a fish on it, all the lines pulled straight back, and the bells Cable had tied on the day before were all ringing. He pulled in fish as he had never pulled before, stopping only long enough to put a call into John. It would be dark in four hours. That would give them time to put a good evening bite in their fish hold.

"Thanks, Cable! We're on our way."

Soon after John arrived, the wind picked up to fifteen

knots out of the northwest, and by evening, it was twenty-five knots, with eight-foot seas. *Tulla*'s fish hold was almost full, and the deck was loaded up to the gunwales as he got ready to head for home. John was finishing up as well and said he would follow Cable in. This last little clatter had filled the *Orford Reef* up also.

Cable smiled. He iced and threw down the last of the fish while the old Wood Freeman autopilot took them home. Grandpa would be happy he had helped their friend find some fish.

Tulla made good time, even with the heavy load. Cable had been taught that was because she was a double-ender, meaning pointy at each end. Running through the night, they would be home by early morning.

John caught up to him around midnight. His boat was faster, so he went on ahead.

"John, could you give Amy a call, please? She and her mom are helping check on Grandpa for me. Maybe he's back at the shack already."

"Sure, Cable. Be glad to. You going right back out?"

"Yup, that was good fishing. I need fuel, grub, and ice though, and a quick check on how Grandpa's doing. *Tulla* and I will go back out tomorrow night."

"That sounds about right for us also."

"See you then."

"Good traveling is what your grandpa would say."

The weather continued to come up, making it a following sea for the remainder of the trip. With the stabilizers out and *Tulla* having a double end, the swells would come up from behind and meet her stern, which would slice through the waves just like the bow would. And all the fish weight kept the side-to-side roll down, so it was a very comfortable ride.

Chapter 6

Cable sat in the helm seat and rested his chin on his chest for a few minutes of sleep. The sun broke over the horizon, painting all the clouds in pink. It was a favorite time for Cable, although the pink clouds did give him a warning. Grandpa had always said, "Pink clouds in the morning, sailors take warning." *Looks like it's gonna blow, so going in is perfect timing.* By the time the blow was over, he'd have his fish sold, fresh supplies on board, and be on his way back out.

The sun was now a big ball of orange-red over the coast hilltops, and the swells were pushing him along toward home.

As he pulled under Mitchell's hoist to unload his fish, Mitchell sent two of his hands down the ladder to unload for Cable, knowing he had been running all night. With *Tulla* tied to the piles, the wave surge wasn't that bad. He saw Amy up above at the edge of the dock and climbed up to get his hug and a Grandpa report.

"Hi there, fisherman," Amy said, smiling ear to ear.

"Hi, Amy. How is he doing?" he asked, giving her a lingering bear hug.

"They're still keeping him. Every other day, Mom and I drive into town to check on him. He's in good spirits. I don't think you can get that man down."

"This is good."

Cable was so tired he was numb as they walked toward the fish scale. "Cable, they're talking about sending him to the VA home in Coos Bay."

"No, they can't do that. He needs to come home to our shack. I can take care of him."

"Cable, he needs special care. If you're out fishing or going to school, who would be there for him? I would help, but I need to help Mom and Dad at the store. And I have school, just like you."

He watched all his fish getting unloaded, wishing Grandpa could see it. "I guess you're right," he said, a heavy weight settling on his chest.

"Nice fish! How many did you get?" Amy asked.

"A boatload. Grandpa said it's bad luck to count your fish before you sell 'em."

Amy smiled, nodding in agreement.

For a thirty-eight-foot boat, *Tulla* could really pack them in. The tally was close to eighteen thousand pounds by the time all the fish were unloaded.

"Amy, when I get a checking account next trip, I want to settle our account with your folks' store. Could you get me the amount, please?"

"Of course. Are you hauling *Tulla* out of the water?"

"Yes. Could you and your mom take me to see Grandpa for an hour? Then I need to buy grub and fuel and head back out. Guess I could take an extra minute for a shower too."

Once unloaded, *Tulla* was hauled and put on her trailer. Cable got her fueled up, made arrangements for more ice, and then talked to Jan about when to put *Tulla* back in the water again.

John and his wife, Alisha, were working on the *Orford Reef* to ready her to go back out. "John, you'll to be ready to run this evening?"

"You bet, Cable. You going in to see Phil?"

"Yes and then right back out for the tuna grounds."

"Sounds good. We'll be ready when you get back. Tell Phil hello for us."

Cable and Amy walked up to the store holding hands. Amy liked to do that. She took Cable's hand whether he wanted to or not. Cable was so tired, he was thankful for the support just to hold him up. Her mom was ready to go, except for the discussion that the ladies didn't want to smell old fish in the car all the way into town and back.

Amy had brought a fresh change of clothes down from the shack earlier that morning after Alisha had called to tell her Cable was on his way in.

Cable showered and changed at the store, climbed in the backseat, and slept all the way to the hospital. When they arrived, Amy woke him up so they could go in together. Grandpa was in good spirits and wanted to hear everything that had happened on the trip. He especially liked the numbers.

The hour went by quickly, and then it was time to go.

"Cable," Grandpa started, "day vaunt me to go da the

VA home. That vould be good tinking. I know you can take care of yourself, and you have Amy here—ve know she is your guardian angel—and the Berquists. Ve already talked about dis."

"No, Grandpa. I can take care of you at our shack. I'll have a bathroom built on and put in a shower, okay?"

"Not right now. Ve'll see. Maybe later, depending if I get better. Now, Cable, you better go catch some more tuna."

"Okay. But I will have a bathroom built for you at the end of the season."

"All right. Now get going, Grandson. Yaw you have more fish to catch."

Cable silently climbed in the car. He was sound asleep again until they reached the store. Amy opened the back door and touched his shoulder to wake him.

"Thanks, Amy. I need some supplies. Then I'll finish icing *Tulla* and put her back in the water. Thank you for the ride, Mrs. Berquist. Put the gas on my bill, please. I told Amy, when I come in next trip, I'll get a checking account and settle up."

"Yes, Cable, that will be fine."

When all the groceries were bagged up, Amy's dad suggested he go with them with the grocery cart, as he wanted to see Cable off.

Mother spoke up. "I want to go too."

So they hung a sign that read "back in 30 minutes" on the store window.

While walking to the boatyard, Dad said, "Cable, you

keep an eye peeled. She's going to blow the next day or so. This could be a big summer storm, like we always have."

"Thanks for that. I saw the pink skies while running in this morning. That's not good."

"All the same, be careful. *Tulla* is a fine sea boat, and your Grandpa taught you well. Amy, Mother, and I worry about you all the same."

"Thank you. You know, the funny thing is, I worry about you here on the beach like you worry about me on the water," Cable said with a smile.

They all had a good laugh.

Standing next to *Tulla* hanging in her slings ready to be lowered in to the water, Cable looked at Amy's folks and said, "Thank you, Mom and Dad." This was the first time he'd called them that, and he meant it.

Amy was thinking it was about time. He was part of their family after all.

"Thank you, Amy. Could I bother you for one of those hugs now?"

"Absolutely, yes you can," Amy smiled.

They did more than hug. Amy gave him a full-size, adult embrace, and a little tear rolled down her cheek. Amy was soon to be sixteen, and being with Cable stirred up new feelings in her.

One minute she felt vulnerable, then the next she felt invincible standing close to him. *God give me strength to say goodbye without turning into a blubbering idiot. He is so wonderful and so mine.* "You be careful," she said.

He smiled and nodded.

It felt good, Amy thought, to hug a full-grown man of

her choosing. *So young, but so old and wise. I know Mom and Dad can see that Cable and I are growing closer all the time.* They were all standing at the edge of the wall as Cable put on his lifejacket and hopped aboard *Tulla*.

Cable signaled he was ready, and Jan lowered away. Cable moved *Tulla* out of the way once in the water so John could come in right behind him. They waved goodbye to their families, and the two boats ran west to the tuna grounds as they had so many times before.

CHAPTER 7

All night, *Tulla* and the *Orford Reef* ran together, out to the fishing grounds, slowing to six knots at daylight to put their gear in the water. Fishing was slow, so they moved northwest and found the school and most of the fleet by noon.

The bite was fast and furious, with fish everywhere. Their decks were quickly loaded, and it was time to ice those beauties down. Cable had to stop icing twice to pull fish. His course was still northwest, pointing toward the main fleet. The wind was starting to howl in the rigging, so to make a course, he would buck up against the wind and swell, slow down, and then turn into the wind and increase to tuna speed. This was a lot of work, but he kept catching while all the other boats slowed to jog and stopped fishing altogether, to drift.

That night, Mother Nature got serious and really blew. *Tulla* swung her stern into the swell and wind and rode like a duck in a windy pond.

On the radio, some boats talked about a hundred to two hundred fish caught today.

Cable called, "John, you there? Come in."

"Yes, Cable. Looks like we got more weather coming for a couple of days. Don't think I'll fish, maybe drift mostly. With our little boats, it's just too hard to make the speed we need. How about you?"

"I would like to fish. That would be all downhill and then a tough buck back up the hill. Not sure it's worth all the wear and tear, Grandpa would tell me. So we'll see."

"Okay, talk to you in the morning. I can see your mast light. A lot of boats are going in to sell while she blows."

"I'm good for now. Talk to you in the morning."

The wind screamed in the rigging all night long; Cable guessed maybe fifty to sixty miles per hour. The hatches were lashed down, and Cable had to wedge himself in his bunk with an extra pillow to keep from rolling out.

He got up during the night to check everything. The wind was still howling, and all was secure. When daylight showed up, he saw gray skies and foam-swept seas. He guessed it was still blowing forty-five miles per hour. The swells had built through the night for combined sea swells of twenty to twenty-five foot, not a good day for fishing. Cable went back to sleep for another four hours.

"John, you there?"

"Yeah, Cable. Where you been?"

"Sleeping. I don't think I can keep the gear in the water, it's so rough."

"Yeah, me too. Say, you wouldn't have an extra Jabsco pump impeller, would you?"

"Yeah, I think so. Maybe a two-inch. We replaced ours this spring. I have the old one we took out. Would that work for you?"

"That should work. I should've done that on mine. The rubber blades are half gone. Not sure I can make it home."

"No problem. Give me your loran numbers. I can run this one over to you." Longitude and latitude showed John was only five miles downwind of him. Cable decided to fish his way over to John.

To his surprise, he was catching fish on the close jigs, next to the boat. *This is strange. The fish must be under the boat even with this weather.*

"John, I put the impeller in a garbage bag and blew a bunch of air around it. I'll come up alongside and then cut across your bow, so you can pick the bag line up with a boat hook. When you have it, I'll let go of the line. Grandpa has done this a bunch of times. He even sent a newspaper over to a friend one time."

Cable brought *Tulla* about twenty feet from John's boat. His son was on the deck with a boat hook, ready to grab the line as Cable dropped it in the water and steered across the *Orford Reef*'s bow.

The operation went as planned. Doing this maneuver at seventy miles out at sea could do some real damage if Cable misjudged maneuvering *Tulla*.

Waiting to hear from John, he jogged *Tulla* next to John's boat as the storm pounded away at the men and their boats.

Finally, the radio crackled. "Cable, it worked!" Smoke was coming from John's engine exhaust.

"I can't thank you enough. You're a chip off your Grandpa's block for sure."

"You're welcome, John. Coming over the five miles to you, I caught twenty or so fish. Think I'm going back that way."

"Okay. Jeez, kid, you're tough. Don't push *Tulla* too hard. Remember, don't start pounding the cotton out of her seams."

"No, I won't do that. Follow me. I'll quarter the sea. You can make tuna speed. Watch."

Off they went, and as soon as they put the gear back in, they were pulling fish. It was a good day. If Cable were a counting man, he would have counted close to a hundred tuna. It was a lot of work, going up the hill and then surfing down the waves, always watching for a wave that might slam into the hull or break over the deck. *Tulla* was a true friend, always taking care of him—especially on Cable's first two trips all alone.

"How's your day, John?"

"Great! Got a hump, maybe a hump and a half."

Cable thought, *That would be 100 to 150 fish. That's real good fishing. We both have about the same.*

John continued, "If it weren't for you, we wouldn't have anything. I think I'm going to just follow you around, Cable. Thanks again for your impeller. We'd still be there, sitting, waiting for a tow or parts. I won't forget it."

"No problem. Grandpa taught me we all need to watch out for each other. We're friends, John."

Dinner was simple—alone, with the storm raging outside and the radio crackling inside. Most all of the fleet had run into port, and the rest were heave-to, riding the blow out. Cable's plans were to keep fishing until she was filled up. "Bandon will be where we're delivering next, *Tulla* girl."

Cable was happy working alone. There were times he would think about Amy's warm, brown eyes and her soft hand in his. *She is a beautiful girl. Wish I was a couple years older. I do think she certainly deserves more than me.*

The next morning as the gray skies gave up some daylight, Cable put his fishing gear in the water, the same way as he had yesterday. The storm had scattered the fish, but they were hungry and hit the jigs with a vengeance.

The fishing was steady, not all at once, but steady all day. He kept working his way north. "We'll have to sell in Coos Bay if we keep this up," he told *Tulla*.

"Cable, got a copy?"

"Yes, John. What do you think?"

"Tomorrow the weather will go down, and they'll school up for us."

"That sounds good. This has been hard fishing."

"Ya, just one more day, and it'll turn westerly to knock down that northerly chop."

They slugged it out the rest of the day. Around midnight, the wind dropped to ten miles an hour and went to the west like John had said it would.

Cable woke in his bunk, feeling the change. What a relief. It was like Mother Nature had given them a gift. Up early, they were still with the fish, and they had schooled up, again like John said. Cable fished as fast and as hard as he could.

The weather had all but completely died down. By nightfall, the fish hold was full.

"John, I'm full. I'm going into Charleston to sell and resupply."

"Okay, We'll run with you. I still need those engine parts."

"Are you going to call Mrs. Dill?"

"Yes, why?"

"Could you get her to call Amy at the store? She likes to keep track of me."

"Not like you aren't enjoying the attention."

"Well … it's like family, you know. She keeps track of Grandpa for me while I'm out here."

"Okay. Alisha can give her a call for you. I'm just giving you a bad time."

"Thanks. I'm heading in there now."

They ran through the night again and, as the sun started coming up, had calm seas and clear skies. Cable could see small puffs of smoke on the horizon. The fleet was running full bore for the tuna grounds. John visited with the group from home, telling what they had done and how Cable saved him—passing over an impeller and then finding the fish.

They arrived in Charleston that afternoon and sold their fish. Mrs. Dill came down to the dock with a nice-looking girl beside her. *Hey, that's Amy with her.* He finished putting the fish hatch cover back on *Tulla*. Amy walked up to the boat as Cable hopped off on the dock.

She said, "Hey there, fisherman. How about one of those hugs?"

"For you, lady, you can have two!"

She smiled as they wrapped their arms around each other. He stood holding her longer than ever before.

"I was worried about you when the storm came. Alisha said you really helped John with engine parts, and then you found the fish."

"Well, maybe. We're good neighbors looking out for each other. How is Grandpa?"

"He's okay. They moved him to the VA home here in Coos Bay, only ten minutes away. When you and John are ready, we can go see him."

"Good. I've been thinking about him a lot."

"Cable, you realize he will probably have to stay there?"

Cable felt his breath leaving him, like a weight was landing on his chest. "I don't like it, but I understand that might be best for Grandpa. I could live on *Tulla*, here, and see him every day."

"You …you mean, you wouldn't live in Port Orford?" she asked, her voice heavy with disappointment.

"No, that's my home. I don't know what I'm thinking. This is such a shock to have him laid up, forever."

"I know it's hard. He was so happy and strong before."

"Thanks for understanding, Amy." He reached over and took her hand.

Grandpa was in good spirits and happy to talk to John about Cable. Cable sat there quietly holding Grandpa's hand. Amy was at his side, and she could tell he wasn't handling it very well, watching his hero and mentor wasting away. She handed him a tissue for his eyes.

Cable stood up, and Amy said to the others, "Excuse us, please. We'll be right back."

She followed him outside and over to a bench. Still standing, fighting back tears, he said, "I guess when you get old, everything goes to pieces on you, like an old boat. Then it just don't float anymore. You know what I mean?"

"Yes, Cable. I know what you mean. It's sad but true."

They sat on the bench. Amy put her arm around Cable's shoulders to comfort him.

They went back in so Grandpa could hear all about the trip. He might've had a stroke, but there was nothing wrong with his mind. He knew what his young man was going through and made it as easy on him as he could.

When they were leaving, Grandpa said, "Vill you give me your hand, Amy? I vaunt to tank you for being my grandson's guardian angel. You're doing yust a fine job. Tank you."

She bent over and hugged him. "You're welcome, Grandpa."

Back at the boats, both John and Cable needed grub and gas. The plan was for everyone to go out to dinner.

Cable made one stop at a bank to set up a checking account and deposited the checks he'd gotten for the last two trips. That done, he handed Amy a five thousand-dollar check to give to her parents; that would pay his and Grandpa's store account bill.

After dinner, the girls informed the men they weren't leaving this evening. They wanted some time together with their men. Amy and Cable sat together quietly on the fish hatch cover and enjoyed the starlit evening. Amy took Cable's arm and pulled it around her shoulders.

Cable spoke first, "I never realized I was your man, as to what was said over the dinner table."

"Well, yes. You are my guy. You've always been there for me and me for you, right?"

"Yes, you're right. Someday a rich, older guy will come along and sweep you off your feet."

"I'm not so sure about that, my fisherman. I like our friendship, and you're very nice. Most of all, Cable, you are faithful to the end, and I like that about you."

"I don't know what I'd do without you. Your mom and dad, all of you, have always been there for me. Thank you."

The summer evening turned cool with the ocean so close. Cable gave Amy Grandpa's bunk, and he slept in his old bunk. It was nice having Amy on board. Maybe someday she would like to come fishing with him. That would be a lot of fun.

They were up before dawn, ready to go. Cable fixed breakfast and checked with John to get going. Hugs were given and gotten, and the ladies left.

Cable pulled out first, excited to catch more fish. He wasn't sure why he hadn't left last night. Amy could have fished with him. Then they could have left right away, instead of sitting at the dock having dinner and hanging around. He didn't feel right being on shore when there were fish out there to catch.

John's son went home with Alisha to get ready for school. She reminded Cable not to be late when school started. Of course, Amy chimed in with her two bits, reinforcing what Alisha had said. She wasn't scolding him, just reminding him not to get carried away and keep fishing. Amy knew he was certainly capable of doing that; it was just in him. That was one of the things she so admired in him.

CHAPTER 8

The month of August flew by. John and Cable met the ladies at Westport, Washington, after fishing their way up the coast. Cable had grown into the position of captain very well. He and John made good fishing partners, and they'd had a good season together.

When Amy and Alisha arrived, they had a serious, sit-down talk with Cable. Alisha was a high school English teacher at the school where Amy and Cable were students.

"Cable, you need to think about getting back to school now," Amy said, gently nudging Cable. "It will be starting soon. We don't want them mad at you, do we?"

Cable's jaw set as he looked at her, considering. "No, we don't."

That was it. He was done talking about it. Amy knew it. She led Cable off to a park bench by the head of the dock. "Cable, I know you don't want to talk about it, but we have to."

She saw him smile as he reached over and patted her knee. He looked like his thoughts were definitely offshore. "You're wanting to keep chasing the tuna all the way up to Cape Scott off the north end of Vancouver Island, aren't you?"

He turned to her, indecision in his eyes.

She continued, "I swear, being alone out there in that boat makes you more antisocial every day, doesn't it?"

He nodded. "I don't have anything to say. I don't want to make you mad at me."

"I know, Cable. I want you home where I can see you every day. You mean a lot to me. And I want you to be there for school. We both need school. Our whole life will be better for it."

"You won't like hearing this," he replied, "but I think my life is pretty good right now. Fishing with *Tulla*, being my own boss. I like it out there alone for ten days. I'm happy. But I do miss you, Amy. You are my best friend."

"Me, the boat, and a few dolphins to keep us company. That's a lot of peace for me. Sitting in class is boring. I don't want to be there. I want *Tulla* rigged up to pot-fish Dungeness crab. They can't teach me that in school."

"No, that's not the point."

"What is the point then? I made more in one month than any of those teachers could make in a year."

"That's still not the point."

"Give me one more trip, and I'll come home. I can work my way south, stop in front of the Columbia River, and then come on home—*Tulla* and me. You do realize I don't like this. It's hard to stop. If it wasn't you asking me, I'd never stop."

"I know that. Someday you'll thank me for it."

"I'm not so sure, pretty girl."

She smiled and squeezed his hand.

The ladies headed home to Port Orford. Cable and John fished a few days out in front of Westport, but it was slow.

"John, I'm going to start south for home. Alisha says the school will be mad at me if I'm late. Not only that, Amy will kill me. Are you staying?"

"One more day, Cable. I'll catch up to you west of the Astoria Canyon, okay?"

"Ya, see you there. Good traveling to you."

By the next morning, the wind and seas were slowly building. Black-gray skies were followed by heavy sheets of rain. The wind came straight out of the southwest and blew through to the north. Fishing was spotty at best. Swells were building to twenty-five-footers with not much of a backside, which made them very steep.

That night, Cable was still fishing in front of the Columbia River. The weather was bad, but not bad enough to go in yet. "Tomorrow we'll go home," Cable said to *Tulla*.

First thing in the morning, the gear went out like it had so many times before. Heavy, dark clouds filled the sky. *There's pink in those clouds, and that ain't good.*

"John, you there?" he called.

"Yeah, I'm almost up to you, Cable. Let's fish our way home, okay?"

"I'm okay with that. Let's do it."

He could see John come up on his side in the early morning light. Mother Nature was starting to blow thirty-five or so now, and the swells were getting bigger. Then the fish decided to eat before the storm.

All the lines loaded up and didn't stop until dark. After getting the last of the fish put away, Cable called John on the VHF.

"This is the first of the equinox, I would say."

John said, "Okay, do we run or stay? That was good fishing today. I hate to run from them."

"Me too. *Tulla* is riding good, but the storm will blow us off the fish."

"I think maybe we need to jog uphill for the night. You good with that, Cable?"

"Yeah, I'm good. These are big enough seas. Grandpa always made me time them out before making my turn. Be careful, John."

"Oh sure. This isn't a problem for the *Orford Reef*. She's a big little boat."

Cable timed the swells like Grandpa had taught him and made the turn with no problems.

John was late in his turn. The boat was broadside and hit hard by the top of a huge wave that broke above the *Orford's* wheelhouse. It didn't stand a chance with the massive weight of the water. The *Orford Reef* took a gut-wrenching roll hard to port.

Everything in the wheelhouse went flying as John jumped upward, fighting to keep his balance. He landed flat-footed on the port bulkhead and prepared himself for the boat to roll completely over. The roll buried the port pole under the wave and put all the port gear into the water.

As the boat righted herself, the port pole shattered under the weight and sudden change of direction. John heard the awful tearing sound and saw the splintered wood, twisted metal, and shredded lines. The pole was dragging all its rigging, heavy, tangled and torn, in the water.

Things were happening too fast. John still expected her to go over and didn't think to pull the engine out of gear. The propeller kept turning, catching one line and then another, wrapping everything around the shaft at lightning speed. The engine screeched to a halt and died. The *Orford Reef* was laid heavy to her port side and was being driven by the wind up the next huge swell, helpless, and completely dead in the water.

John knew this was it. She would go over this time, and there was no coming back. He grabbed the VHF radio, and while reaching for his life jacket, yelled, "Cable, help!"

The radio came alive just before the boom of the wave, and Cable heard John's voice mixed with the sound of busting glass, rushing water, and then silence. As the *Orford Reef* rolled over, the heavy waves smashed the remaining cabin windows inward. Cable's stomach tightened. He knew his friend was in real trouble.

Keeping calm, he searched the water where the *Orford Reef* had been. A small light popped up out of the water and immediately disappeared behind another large swell. *That has to be a lifejacket light.*

Timing his turn again, Cable and *Tulla* clawed their way around the huge swell and got downwind of the light.

Cable shined his spotlight on the small light and could see John in the water struggling to pull on his lifejacket.

Tulla was well downwind now. Cable fought to keep the small spotlight on John as they worked their way back up to him. The *Orford Reef* was gone.

Tulla was a real sea boat. She held steady when Cable steered to put John alongside her, on the inside of the pole stabilizer. This was tricky to do. Setting the autopilot, Cable ran out on deck and threw a line out to John. He grabbed the line and Cable pulled him to the side of *Tulla*. Just then, a swell gave her a heavy roll as Cable reached for John, allowing Cable to pull him over the rail into his arms.

"We got ya, John."

Fighting to keep their balance, they worked their way back into the cabin. John was already shivering and quickly changed into some of Cable's dry clothes. Cable kept *Tulla* heading into the seas.

"Who would've ever thought that could happen so fast? The *Reef* has been a good boat. I'm guessing a freak wave." John said.

Cable just nodded and was glad he could be there for his good friend.

The night dragged on as Cable carefully stemmed the swells nose on. About every tenth wave was larger than the others. It would break at the top of the swell, slam down on the foredeck of *Tulla*, and crash on the side of the cabin.

John was exhausted and lay down in the spare bunk.

Daylight finally came and, with it, an ugly ocean. John

crawled out of the bunk and sat by the stove. He stared out the window as he held a mug of coffee in his hands. "You want to look around for the *Orford*?" Cable asked.

"No," John said in a dazed voice. "She rolled over hard as I stepped off. She was gone on the backside of the wave. They were huge, Cable."

"I think maybe we need to run you into Astoria. It would be too much of a buck for you to make it home," Cable suggested.

"Let's head in closer to shore," John said. He was feeling the finality of losing his boat and his livelihood. "We might be able to beachcomb our way up to the Coos River bar. Then we can make it in there."

Cable said nothing. He understood the pain and frustration of losing a boat. It was like losing a family member.

Chapter 9

They ran for two days against angry seas until they could pull into Charleston, the same place they'd sold earlier in the season. Amy, Alisha, and the kids were standing on the guest dock waiting for them.

Cable landed *Tulla* and dropped John off to be with Alisha. They hugged each other tightly on the dock, his family thankful to have him back well and alive. It was a hard time for the family, with the complete loss of their boat, the *Orford Reef*.

Amy helped Cable tie up *Tulla* for the night. Tomorrow he would take her home to Port Orford for a well-deserved rest on her trailer.

Alisha walked over and hugged Cable. "Thank you, Cable, for bringing him home to us. We can't thank you enough."

"Alisha, we're good friends, just helping each other out. That's the way I was raised. I'm proud to call you and John my friends. We were lucky, or blessed, that *Tulla* and I could be there for John when he needed us."

John walked over and hugged Cable. "I'll never forget what you've done. Thank you, friend."

The storm was slowly wearing itself down. Tomorrow would be a good day for the run to Port Orford. Amy's mother had said she could stay on the boat and keep Cable company on the ride home.

The docks were quiet that afternoon, as if the whole world knew that a boat had been lost. John and Alisha said their goodbyes and left for home. Amy was quiet, wanting to give Cable space to think.

Cable stayed outside, working on his fishing gear. He stood in the troll cockpit in the stern of *Tulla* and put the tuna jigs away for the season. He wrapped them in treated brown paper and placed them neatly, one by one, in the shoeboxes, like Grandpa had him do so many times before.

Amy came outside and sat on the hatch a couple feet in front of him. "Cable, would you like to talk about what happened?"

"No, Amy. I'm okay. I think you'd like to talk about it though."

"Yes, you're right. I can't help but think that could have been us standing there on the dock holding each other."

"No, I don't think so. I'm not cocky, but I am confident. Grandpa taught me better. You need to time your turns, or it will have you, like it did John. Now don't get me wrong; there are freak waves out there, and if your name is on it, you're gone. Look how long Grandpa was out there. He could have died many times, even when he was a cabin boy in the North Sea."

"Cable, I just don't know. There's so much danger out

there and only one of you. I want you safe. I don't want the mighty Pacific Ocean to take you away from me." Her eyes were misty, and a small tear worked its way out of the corner of her eye.

"Well, okay then. Do you think your folks will let me pump gas at the new store up on Highway 101?" he asked with a big grin.

She stopped herself from scolding him and started laughing. She knew that wouldn't work. This man was built to make his living on the sea. "You wouldn't look right in one of those black, plastic bow ties, huh?"

"Thank you, pretty girl, for the vote of confidence. Just to show you my appreciation, how about you let me buy you dinner uptown tonight?"

"You got yourself a deal, Mr. Fisherman."

They pulled out at daylight on the start of the flood tide. Amy was happy to be with Cable. He was becoming her man more and more. And man he was. She could tell him things that were on her mind, but sometimes that didn't go far. This man knew where he wanted to be and when he wanted to get there. Amy remembered a conversation they'd had years ago. Cable had said this was how he comes, and if she doesn't like the ride, she could get off any time.

Cable was exhausted, as usual. It was only twelve hours to home, and Jan would be waiting to hoist them out of the water. Mitchell would have two hands standing by, ready to unload his last catch. But it all seemed a long way away.

Something was still wrong with Amy. She kept putting her hands all over him. "You okay?" he asked.

"No, I'm not okay. That could've been you instead of John. And I just don't want to lose you to the ocean."

"Like we talked yesterday, you're not going to lose me. Grandpa taught me right, and I can do this, Amy."

She stood behind him with her hands resting on his shoulders. She fought back tears as he steered the *Tulla* over the Coos Bay river bar toward home.

They traveled along with a light wind on their stern, and the time passed quickly. Mitchell had him unloaded in record time, and Jan hauled and loaded *Tulla* on her trailer just before dark. They all knew about John's bad luck and thought it better not to ask Cable about the incident, out of quiet respect. They would learn more later.

Amy's mom and dad came down to meet the boat and were glad to see Cable. They all went up to the store and ate dinner, and her dad wanted to hear how John had lost his boat. Cable was tired and didn't talk much, so Amy filled in the blanks for him.

After dinner, what Cable had been dreading finally had to be done. He had to go to the shack without Grandpa.

"Mom, would you mind if I go up to the shack with Cable?"

"Not at all. I'm sure he could use the company."

For once, the wind wasn't blowing. That was rare around Port Orford. The evening stars were out as they walked up the hill holding hands. Cable sighed, "Nice to see the old place. Is there a contractor around so a bathroom can be added on?"

"Yes, there is. I'll get his number for you. Would you like a telephone installed too? We could call Grandpa every week."

"That's a good idea. You're going to drag me into the modern world whether I like it or not, aren't you?"

She smiled. "Yes, it's time for you to come back to the world of people and the living. You can leave *Tulla* in the boatyard for now. Hey, we need to go to school tomorrow. It's the first day, and you didn't miss any. I'm so proud of you."

The shack was dark, and the sight left a hollow spot in Cable's heart. He missed his grandpa. He was everything to Cable.

Amy left him to his thoughts as he sat in Grandpa's rocker. She gave him a kiss on the cheek and returned home. The next morning, Amy found him there, sound asleep and fully dressed, in the rocker where she'd left him the night before. There was no time to clean up. They had to hurry to make the first class.

School was a hustling, bustling place. Amy was a junior, and Cable was a new freshman. They separated to go to their classes.

***

Shortly after first bell, Amy's friend, Mary, came up to her locker. "Amy, your little brother, Cable …he's sitting in the office, and I don't think it's good. They have him in a chair by the vice principal's office."

"Okay. Thanks, Mary," Amy said, turning to walk to the office.

Cable was there, still wearing his knee boots, dirty clothes, and coat from tuna fishing. The smell wasn't good, and people were acting that way. She walked up to the long counter in the school office. Cable looked up with a sheepish grin, smiled, and gave a little wave.

"Hi. I'm a friend of Cable over there."

The secretary looked over the top of her glasses, frowning. "He needs a bath, and some manners wouldn't hurt either."

"Why, what has he done?"

"He told his English teacher to take a hike when she told him he needed a bath."

"Is that all?"

"No, one of the boys came up, shoved him, and told him he stinks. Cable grabbed the boy by the collar, shook him, and told him it was money he smelled and called him a lazy, good-for-nothing pretty boy.

"He's strong, because then he threw the boy across the room into some desks. That's when the vice principal and two male teachers tried to haul him down here. That wasn't pretty either."

Just then, Officer McKee walked in. "Where is he?"

"Over there in the chair."

He took a seat next to Cable, and they started talking. Amy's eyes clouded up. She wasn't sure what to say and didn't want to cry in front of everyone.

Alisha Dill walked up beside Amy. Cable had asked for her since she was an English teacher and John's wife. "What's he done?" she asked.

The secretary took a long, labored breath; exhaled; and repeated what she's just told Amy.

"Did he hurt anyone?"

"No, and he is strong as a bull. Mostly he didn't want anyone touching him. That's why we called the law on him. He's a wild one."

Amy's resentment flared. "He is not. He is kind and gentle. He even saved Alisha's husband's life out on the tuna grounds. He just isn't very social. It comes from a rough life."

Alisha put her hand on Amy's back. "Maybe you should go to class, honey. I'll work on this. You'll see," she said, smiling.

Amy walked back to her class.

Alisha listened as Officer McKee talked with Cable. "You do any damage, Cable?"

"No, sir. None that I could see. I don't like being called dirty by some milk-toast pretty boy. He even had perfume on. When he grabbed my coat, I tossed him. That teacher, she has a mouth on her too. They think they can kick a person who works for a living, sir."

"I heard he grabbed your coat?"

"Yes, sir."

"Why didn't you take a bath this morning?"

"I got in late last night from tuna fishing. Amy didn't want me to be late for the first day of school. Looks like I took care a that, huh?"

"Yeah, let's see if we can sort this out. You stay here. I'll be back."

Pretty boy came into the office and, cruising by Cable,

headed for the vice principal's office. "Your ass is grass, filthy person," he said, taunting Cable.

Cable started coming out of the chair. Officer McKee heard him, along with Alisha.

Cable looked at them and decided sitting down was a better choice as the pretty boy shot into the vice principal's office.

The door closed. After a while, pretty boy came out with his slicked-back hair and Van Heusen button-down collar shirt. He didn't look at Cable but just went on by. The office door closed again, and Cable could hear a lot of talking going on.

The vice principal came out, glanced at Cable, and walked over to the secretary. "Would you please send a runner for Amy Berquist? I need to see her in my office, please."

The secretary nodded, checked the list, and dispatched a runner.

Amy came back into the office shortly. Cable smiled and waved.

She stared at him, shaking her head. "Not happy, huh," he said with a smile as she went into the vice principal's office and closed the door.

The talking continued. Cable had had enough. *This is stupid.* He stood up and said to the world, "I'm going to go see Grandpa. He'll know what I should do."

He'd started toward the door when Amy and the vice principal walked out of the office.

The secretary immediately ratted him out. "He's walking," she said.

"Bag. What a collection of jerks this place has. I never had this problem with Amy or *Tulla*."

The vice principal looked Cable over. "Hold on, Cable. Who is *Tulla*?"

Amy spoke up. "*Tulla* is his and his grandpa's fishing boat. That boat saved John Dill's life with that fourteen-year-old running it a hundred miles out in the Pacific Ocean. Alisha and I seem to be the only people who realize what a good, caring human being is standing in front of us."

The vice principal said, "Oh."

Amy walked over and put her hand under his arm. "Come on, Cable," she said, leading him out. "Let's go find you a bath and some fresh clothes. We'll see if you can survive in this civilized world."

They stopped at the shack, and Cable found some clean clothes Amy had washed while he was out fishing. At Amy's house, she sent him to the shower and explained to her folks what had happened. "I think he scared those two teachers and the vice principal. All of them kept their distance for sure."

"Oh my. What are you going to do, Amy?" Mom asked.

"I'm not sure. Alisha will be our best help. This is something that hasn't come up before. If he doesn't go to school, they'll send a truant officer for him, haul him off to juvenile hall, and lock him up. Officer McKee said it's all downhill from there. I don't want that, Mom. I care for him too much to let that happen."

Freshly scrubbed and dressed, Cable came out of the bathroom and looked at the folks and Amy. "In goes the dirty, and out comes the clean," he said with a big grin on his face.

"Come on," Amy said. "You need to comb your hair. We'll get it cut as soon as we can. Cable, sometimes …"

They all started laughing to relieve the tension before Amy and Cable went back to the school.

"Amy, I'm sorry if I embarrassed you and your folks. I just wasn't going to take that smart-mouthed pretty boy grabbing my coat."

"I know, Cable. But sometimes you have to put up with a few things."

"You mean like smart-mouthed pretty boys and teachers who look down their noses at you?"

"Yes, sometimes."

"Just not so sure about that, pretty girl."

They went back to the vice principal's office to see what was next. "We need you to go to the library, Cable. Then after school, there'll be a meeting for all who are involved."

"Okay. Will Amy be there?"

"We'll see."

"If she isn't, don't look for me."

"You don't order me, young man."

"No, sir, not ordering you. Just telling you where I'm at. Your choice." Cable didn't crack a smile. He looked straight at the vice principal.

"All right." He sighed. "Amy, you be sure and be here."

When they walked out, Cable looked at Amy. "Are they going to send me to Veda? At least if Burley wants to hit me, I can hit him back."

"Cable, stop talking like that. We'll see. I just don't know. See you at lunch in the cafeteria."

"Okay. I'll be there."

In the cafeteria, they sat side by side. A lot of the girls were checking out the new freshman. He looked real good to them, and Amy knew it. "Cable, this is serious. They could send you to an orphanage. You and Veda have history."

"I won't stay there. I won't run away. I'll just walk out the front door and come home to the shack and *Tulla*."

"I know that. That's part of the problem. They could send you to juvenile hall. That's jail. And you wouldn't do so well there."

They sat quietly finishing their lunch. "Amy, why do those girls keep looking at me and smiling? Do they want something?"

"Oh yes. But I don't think it would interest you right now."

"How would you know that?"

"You already have a girl, and her name is *Tulla*."

Cable thought awhile. "Yeah, you're right about that. How is it you're always right?"

"You trust me. That's why."

All afternoon, Cable was in the library watching out for Amy.

He talked to the librarian and asked if he could help somehow. She showed him how to use the Dewey Decimal System and gave him a cart of books to reshelve. Cable worked nonstop. Then he asked for another cart of books.

It was fun. He read the titles as he put the books on the shelves.

Amy had study hall last period and got to the library with a pass. She came in looking for him, and the librarian pointed her toward the back. "He's been a delight to have in the library. He works quietly and has very few questions. I would like to keep him for one of his class periods."

Amy smiled. "That's an idea."

They went to the office together and were sent straight to the conference room. As they sat at the table waiting for everyone else, Cable said, "Amy, I don't like it here. This is some kind of a ramshackle deal coming at us."

She smiled at him and nodded. "We need to do this, Cable."

Cable sat quietly. Amy opened one of her books and flipped through the pages.

The vice principal walked in with two strangers and the secretary carrying a pencil and pad. Alisha came in as soon as the final bell rang.

After the door was closed, Officer McKee walked in, apologizing for being late.

The vice principal spoke up first. "Thank you all for coming. All of you know why you are here. For the record, it is for the care and supervision of one Cable Dent."

He then named all who were present and their interest in the meeting. "Cable had an incident this morning where hygiene was in question, and that led to an incident of violence. The school position is that violence will not be tolerated."

Alisha immediately spoke up, "I thought that was

resolved with a bath, and the incident was provoked. So why are Social Security and the truancy officer here? And, why the county sheriff?"

Alisha was not happy. Officer McKee raised his hand. "If I might please …"

The vice principal nodded to him.

"I asked to sit in to provide some background for the hearing. Cable's dad, Ben, and I went to school together. He was a nice guy, but he went to drinking after coming back from the war, and we parted ways.

"Ben was a good man. He was raised by his dad in a fisherman's shack down at the marina and went fishing every summer with his dad, Cable's grandpa. Cable is doing that now. Cable's folks, Ben and Carol, were killed in a car accident on Highway 101.

"That was when Cable was eight years old. I had to serve the warrant to release the boy to Veda, Carol's mother. He ran back to his grandpa the same afternoon. Everyone knew they were mean, Veda and her man, that is, and the boy only wanted to live with Phil. All that was good, and everyone knew it.

"Phil had a stroke this summer and went to the VA home in Coos Bay, where he is now. I've visited him. He's worried a lot about the boy, now that he's back from fishing. Then today happened, and here we are."

Alisha raised her hand. "What are you planning to do? He hasn't broken any laws, other than being a minor, and a very responsible one at that. Why would a truant officer be here?" Looking at the truant officer, she continued, "Most importantly, why would the school invite you? Cable is not truant."

Before the vice principal could start talking, there was a knock at the door. And before there was time for an answer, the door opened, and in walked Amy's mom and dad; Jan Kayden, the hoist operator; and Mitchell, the local fishmonger. They went to the chairs lined up against the wall.

Before the door closed all the way, a large boot shoved it open again with a bang. "My name is Dill, John Dill. This man saved my life this summer, and you won't take him from this community without a fight."

Alisha turned and smiled, pointing to the empty chair beside her.

"Thank you for that, Mr. Dill. Social Security, you are here for …?" Alisha asked again.

"The vice principal called us. What I hear and see is that this young man is a stable citizen with many caring friends. We need a supervising adult to sign for him. Would we have any takers?"

Amy stood up. She was immediately followed by her parents, who walked over to stand beside her. Then John and Alisha stood up, followed by a whole wall of people, even Officer McKee.

The Social Security person smiled. "I only need one."

"Ma'am," Amy's dad said, "my family and I have had Cable in our home when he had to go to school and his grandpa left for spring fishing. Cable is like one of our own. We would be more than happy to sign for him. Our home is already his home."

"Well, that certainly works for me," said the Social Security person.

"Cable," the vice principal asked, "do you want to say anything?"

"Yes. I'd like to thank you all for being here as my support. My grandpa would thank you if he were here. The Berquists are like my family. I would be happy to be there, as long as I can sleep in my shack on the hill and go fishing when the fish are running."

They all chuckled at that.

Amy's folks were given an appointment in Coos Bay to become the responsible party for Cable's care.

"Just for the record, we will be investigating one Veda Hackmore. Restitution will be pursued."

Cable raised his hand. "Ma'am, if you get anything back, could it go to my grandpa, please? He has it coming."

"I'll let you know, Cable."

The vice principal was ready to close the meeting. "Looks like we're done here, everyone. Thank you for your time. You all may go now."

Everyone gathered around Cable, shaking his hand and patting him and Amy on the back.

Grandpa's fisherman shack

Gear locker

Port Orford dock and cranes

Boat on hoist

PART 3

PART 3

CHAPTER 10

Life finally settled down. The bathroom was added onto the shack, and a phone was put in. Cable and Amy called Grandpa every Sunday evening. He waited for their calls and always had to say hi to Amy and remind her she was his adopted granddaughter now.

Cable bought all of John's crab pots and worked a deal with the school. Monday to Thursday he was in class, and Friday to Sunday he would pot-fish Dungeness crab.

The school said Friday was Cable's day for industrial arts and work skills development. As time passed, he took one student with him on Fridays to share his experience. This arrangement was good for all, and he learned how to write a lesson plan and report back to the teacher. Then there were weeks at a time when he couldn't get out due to the winter storms.

When Cable couldn't get out fishing, he helped Amy at the store. He stocked shelves and took inventory while Amy minded the till for the folks. In the evenings, they did homework at Amy's or Cable's kitchen table, depending on who was cooking that night.

It was a cold, wet, windy November evening when

Amy was managing the till while Cable stocked shelves and swept the floor. A "pretty boy," as Cable would say, strode through the door sporting a fancy new ski jacket; carefully combed, blond hair; and a suntan right out of a magazine. He blew by Cable in a hurry, bumping him while he was bent over sweeping into a dustpan.

"I need a pack of Kools, darlin'."

"Regulars or extra menthol, sir?" Amy asked politely.

"Well, extra, of course. Say, you're cute. When did you start working here?"

"My mom and dad have owned the store since I was born," she said, smiling back.

"Too bad. You could have a lot of fun in Coos Bay."

"No thanks. I like it here in Port Orford. I have everything I want here," Amy said, smiling again and glancing toward Cable.

"Oh yeah, sure. I bet you don't have any men who can make a little girl as pretty as you satisfied," he said with a sneer.

"Things are just fine here for me, like I said before." Amy stared up at him, not smiling anymore.

Leaning on the counter, he continued, "Hey, honey. I'm just trying to offer a country girl my vast knowledge of pleasure-seeking skills."

Cable was listening and didn't like where this was going. He moved in closer, now sweeping the floor in front of the counter next to the rude city boy.

"I don't like or need any of this talk," Amy said. "Here is your change and cigarettes. Please leave."

"You little snip of a country hick, I'm trying to offer

you a different flavor of pleasure. You get it?" he said, smiling again with a wink.

"Like I said, I don't want it."

Cable stood up tall and stepped in front of the pretty boy, matching him in height and build. Amy could see Cable bristle with anger. The grip on his broom was getting tighter. "You heard the lady, slick. She needs you to move on."

"Jeez, stupid country hicks are coming out of the cracks in the floor," he said loudly and spit on the floor.

Cable leaned his broom up against the counter edge, took his store apron off, and laid it neatly on the counter. He turned back to face the person making insulting remarks.

"Well, stupid country hick, what are you going to do? Throw me out for your country whore here?"

"We may be stupid ..." Cable started to say. His hands, terrifyingly strong and built by years of fishing, moved around the guy's neck in a flash and squeezed. The pretty boy's breath got cut off, and he started to flail his legs and arms. He tried to pull Cable's hands away from his neck as his face turned blue. Cable leaned in close and said calmly into his ear, "But we are strong."

Amy yelled, "No, Cable! No fighting in the store, you two."

Cable smiled slightly. "We aren't fighting. This pretty boy dirty mouth seems to be struggling for some air." Cable stood there, waiting for him to stop struggling.

"Amy, my hands are full right now. Would you mind opening the front door for us? We'll take this outside."

Amy ran around the counter and pushed the front door wide open. Cable was right behind her, half running and pushing the smart mouth backward out the door into the rain and the wind.

Cable saw a Corvette parked in front of the store. He slammed the foul-mouthed person onto the hood flat on his back, knocking the wind out of him even more. Cable's knees came up and pinned his victim's shoulders down on the hood. He released the hold on his neck and heard the bloodcurdling scream as the guy sucked in his first breath of air.

Cable pulled back his fist, took a centerline handful of new ski coat, and started pounding the guy's face. He got in two solid blows and was at the ready for another when, over his shoulder, he heard a familiar voice.

"Cable, don't hit him anymore," Officer McKee said sternly.

There was blood everywhere. Pretty boy's nose was flat on his face, blood streaming out, and a nasty cut above his left eye.

Cable relaxed some but didn't release his target and looked toward the voice.

Officer McKee had been sitting in his car doing paperwork when the two of them came flying out the door. Now he was halfway out of his car.

Cable let go and backed up onto the front porch. Pretty boy rolled over, fell off the hood of the car onto the wet ground, and promptly started throwing up on himself. The rain came down harder, and the wind blew the door open, slamming it back and forth, on the front porch of the store.

Amy ran out and took Cable's arm. She held him tight. Her whole body was shaking with fear of what might happen. Officer McKee kneeled and inspected the victim. "Amy, call an ambulance, please. Cable, you go inside and have a seat."

Pretty boy pushed himself up, put his hands on the car, and continued to spew obscenities even as the officer told him to be quiet. Cable could smell the alcohol on him after all the vomiting he had done.

Cable led Amy inside and closed the door. She picked up the phone to call for an ambulance. He then escorted her to the chairs by the potbelly stove. They sat down and waited. Cable held Amy's hand as he felt the adrenaline slowly draining from his system.

Mom and Dad heard the commotion from upstairs. They came down, went outside, surveyed the scene and came to talk with them.

"Why, Cable?" Mr. Berquist asked. "You didn't have to beat him so badly."

Cable sat there as the wind and rain beat on the window. "I'm sorry, but I won't let anyone talk to Amy that way, not as long as I'm around."

"You could have killed him. Then what, go to jail?" Amy said as tears streamed down her pretty, soft cheeks.

Dad walked over to the door and watched the ambulance finish up and leave with the injured person. Officer McKee came inside and sat down next to Amy. "Okay, what happened?"

She explained it all, even where the guy shoved Cable before Cable grabbed him and drug him to the door for removal.

Officer McKee asked, "Why did you hit him?"

"That was the only way I could take the fight out of him. You see, with all that booze, he was stupid and wouldn't stop.

"I was trying to protect Amy from him. He was making suggestions of sexual … What's that word? Provocative or something like that. Just won't happen with me here. I asked him to leave, but he decided he'd stay and see what'd happen. Guess he found out. Grandpa used to say, 'Never judge a book by its cover.'"

"All right then. Both of you stick around. I need to get to the hospital before he takes off."

"I'm not going anywhere," Cable said with a smile.

Amy looked at Cable. "You didn't have to hit him like that, Cable. It was almost animal like. You were a wild man."

"Amy, I'll protect you to the death. You are more than just a friend. You're like the air I breathe. I can't live without you. There won't be some stranger coming in foul-mouthing the family I love."

Cable stood up and said to the folks, "Excuse me. I think I'd like to go to my shack."

They both nodded and said, "Yes, you do that. We'll let you know when Officer McKee comes back."

CHAPTER 11

Cable walked home, the rain soaking through his clothes as the wind buffeted him about. He wondered if he had just lost his best friend and his family while only trying to protect them. *I wish you were here, Grandpa. Maybe you could straighten me out.*

He walked through the back door of his fisherman's shack. It was dark and cold inside. He turned on the single light bulb that hung over the small, round kitchen table where Grandpa and he would sit.

Grandpa would tell stories of Norway when he was a boy. He'd worked on old sailing ships that hauled coal from Africa to Norway in the dead of winter through the North Sea. Sometimes they'd get caught in storms that made the old wooden ships open up and start taking on water. All hands would go down below to bail water.

He said even the captain was down there bailing water. They all knew they might die. If it wasn't their turn to go to Valhalla this trip, yaw maybe the next trip. Yaw, sure enough, there was a next trip and another after that. Yust like fishing, there is always daw next season.

Guess not though, if you're lying in the VA home.

Probably Valhalla doesn't sound so bad to Grandpa right now.

"What am I thinking?" Cable said aloud to no one. "Why am I thinking this way? Amy is right. I spend too much time alone. I know there'll always be another fishing trip."

And there will always be someone to insult the woman I love. "If anyone does that again, I'll beat them to a pulp if it takes the last breath I draw."

The storm was blowing harder outside, and Cable's anger was not subsiding. He sat in Grandpa's chair and stared out the small bay window into the blackness of the night.

A quiet, distinct tapping came from the door. He looked through the window to the little porch and saw Amy standing in a hooded raincoat, soaking wet. Cable got up and reached to open the door. Amy stayed on the porch. Neither said a word. Finally, Cable said, "Amy, I don't know what to say."

"Don't say anything. Just hold me, please."

He wrapped his man sized arms around her gently, and they stood there a long time in each other's embrace. All the questions about what had happened earlier melted away. Pulling Amy through the door, Cable closed it behind her. Gently, he said, "Here, let me take your coat. Please have a seat. I'll put on some water, and we'll have spiced cider."

She had a tissue in her hand and sniffed quietly as she held it to her nose. Cable fixed the spiced cider, set both mugs on the little round table, and sat in his chair across from her.

He glanced at her, not knowing what to say to fix the broken-ness. His fingers toyed with the handle of the cup. Amy sipped her cider silently, slowly gaining her composure. For now, they didn't have to talk. All they wanted was to be in each other's company, especially after a night like tonight.

Amy finally broke the silence, her voice almost a whisper. "You said a lot when you were leaving tonight."

"I got a little wound up," he replied, "hitting the foul mouth. I apologize for that."

"No. No, Cable. You're right. We are your family, and I love you also. You know, you've never said that to me before."

"I know. I wasn't sure if I could tell you how I really feel. But with the emotion and all, I couldn't help myself. I just had to say it to you."

"You said it. Did you say it like a man tells a woman, or was it like a brother tells a sister?"

There was a long pause as she watched his face.

"Cable, please. I need to know."

"Oh, boy, this is hard. I don't want anything I say or think to come between our friendship. I really need you, and you're my family. There would be a hole in me if you and your folks weren't there."

"Go ahead. Tell me," Amy quietly coaxed him.

He looked at the floor, and then he held up his head with the confidence of a full-grown man. "Amy," he said, "I love you as a grown man would tell a grown woman."

Amy smiled, nodded, and reached across the table to take both of Cable's thick, rough hands in hers. Cable could feel their soft warmth. "I love you also, Cable Dent, as a grown woman would tell a grown man. We are one and the same, Cable. We have been for a long time."

They sat looking into each other's eyes and holding hands. No other words were needed.

Cable pulled his hands away, sat back, and took a sip of cider. "You remember the first day of school?"

She nodded with a little smile.

"I was fishing when I asked you if the girls who smiled and looked at me wanted something. You told me I already had a girlfriend, and my heart did flips. Then you said it was *Tulla*. That wasn't so. I wanted you to be my girlfriend. I know I'm younger than you, and my gut tells me I'm not good enough for you."

"No, Cable. I have known since I found you in the rocks on the jetty, soaking wet, that you were the one. I would love to be your girl. In fact, I have always been your girl."

"Wouldn't people at school laugh at you for having a younger guy? A junior dating a freshman?"

"Don't worry about them. You and I spend more time together than we ever will with them. What they think doesn't matter. It's what you think that matters to me."

"And to me, my girl," he said.

She leaned in her chair and reached for him so they could have one of those hugs. It was nice to spend this quiet time together. And so went the evening.

When it came time for Amy to go home, Cable grabbed their coats. "Wait, I'll walk you," he said. "Can I tell people you're my girl now?"

"Yes, you can. Can I tell people you're my guy?"

"Sure. If you don't, I will. Okay?"

"Yes."

Chapter 12

Not a whole lot changed, as Amy and Cable had already been holding hands in public. Amy wanted a going-steady ring. Cable got Mom to run them into Bandon so Amy could pick one out. Cable liked the ring with two porpoises swimming together. "Just like us, Amy, a couple of porpoises swimming along in life together."

She preferred something without mammals and picked out a simple design. Every so often, Cable would ask her again if a younger guy was okay. Her reply was always the same, "As long as he's this younger guy."

Grandpa was happy to hear they were going steady. He checked out her ring and mentioned that, as far as he was concerned, it could've been a wedding ring. "That isn't quite where we're at," Amy reassured him.

Amy would be sixteen soon, and they both needed transportation. She finished up her driver's training class, and on the Saturday before Christmas she took the test. She passed with flying colors and happily received her driver's license.

"Congratulations, Amy! What say we buy some wheels?"

"Okay, Cable. What do you have in mind?"

"Well …I was thinking we sure could use a pickup truck with all the fishing gear we need to haul around. How about you?"

"I was hoping for a car we could drive to school and make a trip to see Grandpa in Coos Bay now and then."

"How about this? Get the truck first. Then we'll buy you a nice car after the fishing season next year. I really need something to pick up crab pots and gear. That would give me a good truck we could keep forever, and you get a new car when you need one."

She smiled. "Cable, sometimes …"

During dinner with the Berquists, Cable said, "You know, this going steady stuff is getting confusing. Here we are, already buying a truck and all."

Mom said, "Officer McKee stopped by today. He said the rude city boy Cable beat up decided to drop all charges when he fessed up he was drinking."

"That's good. I was afraid Cable would be in trouble," Amy said.

"I hope he's smart enough not to come around here again," Cable chimed in.

On New Year's Day, Cable and Amy were out on the water all day putting out their crab pots. He was happy to be back fishing again, and even though it was a late crab fishing opener for some reason, he would take what he could get. The gear could soak until Friday. He had built a live tank for the crab in the fish hold. That let him fish all weekend and then sell Sunday evening.

Amy was happy. She had her man, a truck with a

license to drive it, and the adventure of fishing with Cable. Come Sunday morning, they pulled gear and checked the pots, taking out a nice catch of crab. The pots went back in the water to soak for a few more hours. They waited until the last minute to pull the gear again, take out the catch, then return to the dock to sell their crab and haul *Tulla* out of the water.

Tulla seemed to like crabbing. That's what the locals called it. She was sea-kindly, and they had their share of crab to sell.

Cable walked Amy home, and Mom was waiting for them at the door. "Cable, the VA home called. It's Grandpa. He's taken a turn in the last day. You might want to go see him now. I'll drive you and Amy into Coos Bay."

"Thank you, Mom. I need to change first. I'll go up to the shack and clean up. If I finish early, I'll walk back your way."

Cable couldn't help but think about Grandpa as he changed clothes and combed his hair. On the ride into town, with Mom driving, Amy sat in the middle and Cable was on her right. Cable wasn't a talkative person, but today he was especially quiet.

"You okay?" asked Amy.

"Yeah, I feel guilty for not spending more time with him."

"I think he understands," Mrs. Berquist said. "He knows there are a few miles between the VA home and your home and work. You've kept as close as you can. And sometimes it's just our time. He's had a great life. You know he's told all of us that many times."

"He told me when Mom and Dad were buried that someday I would have to bury him next to them. I never would've thought this could be the time. It seems too soon. He has given me so much. I think he was the angel watching over me."

"Yes, he is." Amy put her hand on Cable's leg. "He has taught you well, and he is so proud of you. We all are." He patted her hand and gave it a gentle squeeze.

At the front desk, the receptionist said Grandpa was sleeping, but they could go sit with him if they liked.

"Ma'am, is he close to going?" Cable asked.

"Yes, he could be. He's slipped into a coma state, and his vitals have slowed. The doctor said he's close."

"Thank you, ma'am. Yes, we'd like to sit with him if we could, please."

Cable pulled up chairs for the ladies and then one for himself next to the head of the bed, where he could hold Grandpa's hand.

Amy could see the immense pain surging through Cable. He sat there and watched as Grandpa labored to breathe. Cable turned to Amy with tears running down his cheeks. "Amy, this is hard. He gave me everything and asked for nothing in return. What a great man. I am so lucky to have him in my life."

Amy leaned her head against his and said, "He is a gift to have in our lives. We will never forget him."

Still holding their heads together, Cable said, "You know, Amy, when you brought me to the shack during the storm the day we buried my mom and dad, he told me you were like a guardian angel for me. I have never forgotten that. Thank you for being a part of our lives."

Amy nodded, tears welling up in her eyes.

They stayed a while longer and then headed home after making sure the nurse had the phone number for the shack. "Call at any time if there's a change, please."

The ride was quiet going home.

Mom stopped to let Cable out, and Amy said, "Mom, I'd like to go with him."

"Sure, you stay if you like. He could use the company, I'm sure."

It was close to midnight when the phone rang. Amy was lying on the couch under a blanket Cable had covered her with. "Hello," Cable answered. "Yes, ma'am, this is Cable Dent. Yes ma'am, I understand. Yes ma'am, twenty minutes ago. Thank you for calling. Goodbye."

"He's gone Amy. Damn, I'm going to miss that man. He wasn't only my grandpa. He was my best friend, like you."

Amy had stood up and moved close to Cable. She gently wrapped her arms around him. She didn't say anything. She just stood there in the dark, listening to the wind groaning around the corners as it blew down on the little fisherman shack.

Cable didn't have any more tears as he stood there holding Amy. He had already given them up. Grandpa was already where he was going to next, sitting there with new friends and sharing fishing stories about the Pacific Ocean that he so loved to tell.

Cable tried to process all the thoughts running through

his mind. He said, "We need to make arrangements … Maybe Saturday? Guess we'll see. Will the school excuse us so we can make arrangements?"

"I'm sure they will," Amy said. "Tomorrow after school we can skip study hall with a slip and go to the VA. They'll tell us what we need to do."

The next day at school was a long one for Cable, until he met Amy at her wall locker. He helped her with her coat, and they braved the sheets of rain, running to the pickup. The ride seemed to take forever. Amy had to concentrate on the slippery road, so not much was said. Once at the VA Extended Care Center, they signed for Grandpa's personal effects and picked up the plain, simple, brown paper bag that contained them. Cable couldn't stop the dull pain he felt in his heart for Grandpa.

They stopped at the funeral home to make the service and burial arrangements and decided on a Saturday graveside service. Mrs. Berquist said she would put on a reception at the community hall. Amy had brought along a change of clothes out of Grandpa's closet for him. Grandpa would be dressed as he had lived, as a fisherman.

It was dark when they finally started the drive home. "Amy, can we stop at *Tulla* before we go home? I want to tell her that Grandpa's gone. Now we're the last two standing … Then you and I will be one when you take the name Dent."

She reached over and put her hand on his knee. "Cable, you've never said anything like that before."

"Yeah, well. It had to come out sometime. What do you think?"

"Amy Dent … I like it," she said as she patted his leg.

"I've been quietly waiting to hear me called Dent, and you were the first."

At the boatyard, the wind was howling in the rigging, and the rain was still coming down in sheets. Cable got out when Amy stopped the truck and stood next to *Tulla*'s big, wet, windswept hull shining in the headlights of the truck.

He placed his hand on her hull gently as to the true friend she was and leaned his forehead against her. "*Tulla*, it's just us now—you, me and Amy. We're all the family you got now." He patted her hull as the rain continued to pour down. "Grandpa's gone. He loved you, old girl, like Amy and I do. You have a good rest now. We have some fishing to do later."

The truck cab was nice and warm as he climbed back in. Amy had kept the engine running. "She's fine. I told her the three of us have some fishing to do."

Amy smiled and drove to the general store. They got out and ran to the front porch to keep from getting soaked.

Amy's mom had dinner warm and waiting for them. She had seen them drive over to *Tulla*. Looking at Cable, she asked, "Did you tell *Tulla* Grandpa's gone?"

"Yes, I did. That's where I went the day we put Mom and Dad on the hill. I guess we'll say our goodbyes to Grandpa on Saturday."

"I remember," Amy's mom said. "Amy brought a soaking little mouse in out of the weather. Cable, you've grown straight and tall. Your grandpa's to be thanked for that. He did a good job with you, and we're all proud to have you in our family." She smiled and patted him on the shoulder as he sat at the kitchen table.

Chapter 13

For Cable, time crawled the rest of the week. School was almost unbearable, and he could hardly concentrate. But he knew Grandpa would want him to keep up. The best part was the few hours he could steal away to the gear locker.

He had set up an area where he could build crab pots from raw parts with his bare hands and a few tools. It felt good to work. Amy would come fetch him for dinner with the folks. That was family time and then he'd study and head home to the shack.

Friday night Amy asked, "How about a movie in Bandon tonight, Cable?"

"No thanks. You take a couple of your girlfriends. I want to work late and get these pots finished."

She looked disappointed and then smiled. "Hey, I have a new book I've wanted to read. Can I come over and read while you work?"

"Sure. Sounds great."

Amy was keeping close even though Cable wasn't talking much. She knew her guy, and this was a life event

Cable had to deal with. All things were final except for his memories. And tomorrow was the day.

While wrapping rubber on a pot frame, he thought of all the times he and Grandpa had spent in that small space working on gear. *Darn, I miss you, Grandpa. I hope you're okay, wherever you are.*

Saturday morning, Cable wore his best duds as he helped set up the reception hall. Amy was pretty, with her hair fixed and all. Finally, it was time to walk to the cemetery. The caretaker had pitched a shelter next to the freshly dug grave, as the rain was still coming down like it had been all week.

More folks showed up than Cable had thought would come. It looked like most of the Port Orford fishing fleet wanted to pay their last respects. They gave Cable and Amy seats in front. The service wasn't long with the weather as foul as it was.

Cable could only look straight ahead, stoic with the set of his jaw. Amy couldn't help but cry. After they lowered the casket into the ground, Cable walked over to the graveside, scooped up some dirt in his hand, and sprinkled it on the casket. "Goodbye, Grandpa. Good luck wherever you are, and travel safe. Maybe someday you'll see me when you return to Mother Earth from Valhalla."

Amy was at his side with her hand under his arm as they walked slowly toward the community hall.

After saying hello to most everyone, Cable excused himself and walked to the shack. He changed out of his good clothes and put on his fishing boots and coat. Amy showed up shortly at the door. She looked at him. "Boat?"

"Yeah, I just couldn't stand there. *Tulla* needs some company."

"Can I catch up with you? Would you mind?"

"No, not at all. Think I'll fire up her stove to dry things out and maybe put on the teapot."

He walked down to the boats and climbed up the ladder to *Tulla*'s deck. Sliding the cabin door open, he slipped inside and noticed how fast it was getting dark outside as he turned on the single, small, overhead light.

Nothing smelled so good as an old, wooden fish boat. Cable pulled off his boots and coat and started the little diesel stove. He warmed his hands as the stove began to warm up the cabin nicely. *This has been a long week*, he thought. Realizing how tired and drained he was, he slid into the bigger bunk, leaving the small light on for Amy when she got there.

Cable lay in his bunk half-asleep. He liked listening to the rhythm of the rain pounding away on *Tulla*'s cabin roof and the sounds of the wind whistling through her rigging and the riggings of all the other boats in the yard.

Amy came in quietly and closed the door behind her. Off came her boots and coat and then she slid in next to Cable, facing him. He put his arm out so she could nestle her head into his shoulder and pulled the blanket over her. She let out a little sigh of contentment.

"Are you sure you want to hook up with a fisherman for the long haul? I'm not so sure this life is what you'll want."

"Cable, I thought we settled all that. I want to be with you …fisherman, boatman, lumberman, whatever man.

We will do it together. Yes, I am here for the long haul. My name will be Dent someday, and I want it that way." She put her hand flat on his chest and felt the rise and fall of his breathing. "You have any more questions?"

"No, I just wanted to check with you. Thanks for coming to the boat. I think this is what I needed to do."

"This is wonderful being here together, warm and snug and listening to the storm carrying on outside."

They quietly fell asleep in each other's arms.

PART FOUR

CHAPTER 14

On Fridays, Cable took one or two students crab fishing with him, weather permitting. They learned as they rode along. Some couldn't keep their breakfast down but insisted on finishing out the day.

Amy came with him on Saturdays and Sundays, and they were a good team. Amy ran the boat while Cable worked the gear, hauling up the crab pots, taking out the crab, freshening the bait, and throwing the pot back in. Then Amy would drive *Tulla* to the next pot so Cable could do it all over again.

He rigged a couple of twelve-volt tractor lights for deck lights, and that let them fish way past dark. Some evenings, with the heavy rain clouds coming in from the ocean, it was dark by 4:30.

Cable had the pot buoys numbered, so Amy was careful to keep track of where the pots were and record how many keeper crabs were caught. She did all this while running the boat.

They would both get excited when the pots came up full of crab.

Cable laid their gear out in three strings of twenty

pots each. The first string started outside the breakwater running west and then northwest toward the Orford and Blanco reefs. They were exposed to heavy northerly storms and seas. The crabbing was rougher but better out there.

The other two strings were to the south along the coast as far as Island Rock in five to ten fathoms of water. That would be thirty to sixty feet of water he told his "Friday crew" of students. With that setup, if it was too rough to fish the northwest pots, they could fish the ones on the south side.

"Rocky Point, Amy. I want to get in tight and dump some gear in the fifteen to twenty foot holes next to Rett's Creek. It's just south of here."

Amy was sure she had heard him wrong. "You're talking about fifteen to twenty feet? That's right under the highway there, isn't it? I think that's a sheer rock cliff."

Amy continued, "I know the set is north in winter. We know that, right?" She reached for a loaf of bread in *Tulla*'s tiny galley, looking at Cable as if he had lost his mind.

Still questioning, she said, "Right, it's awful shallow in there with certain kinds of weather. You know the rollers come in there?" She did know that Cable knew, but it still didn't make any sense to her why he talked about doing this.

"Yeah, you're right. We get some real boomers there, so here's the plan—"

"Plan? I thought we were just having a conversation, not making a plan."

"No," Cable said matter-of-factly, "a plan. I think there are big holes dug out by the winter storms. The feed and freshwater get trapped in there, and the crab are standing in line to hop in those holes and have dinner."

"Okay …" she answered skeptically.

"So, we swing in there and dump off ten pots Saturday morning. We get them out of there Sunday evening. What do you think, pretty girl?" Cable said, standing up and smiling.

"I'm not sure. *Tulla* is a sweetheart of a boat, but if she sputters once, we'll be on the rocks for sure. I don't like it, Cable." She handed him a freshly made peanut butter and jam sandwich. "Hot cocoa?"

"Yes, please. Okay, I can drop you at the dock, and I'll have it all in the water before dark. Then I can pull the pots just before dark Sunday. That should be enough time to prospect the spots I'm thinking of."

"Oh no. You're not dumping me off at the dock and having all the fun. Besides, you need me to steer *Tulla* and keep an eye on the electronics. If fog comes in, that would call the whole thing off, or a Nor'west twenty-five, right?"

After chewing a big bite of his sandwich, Cable said, "I know the rollers will come in. If it's foggy, you can hear the waves crashing on the rocks way before you see them, so we have a built-in sonar above the water."

"I'm still not liking this," Amy said, shaking her head.

"C'mon, let's try. We could be rich before we know it. You'll see."

She smiled and shook her head. "Cable, sometimes …"

Cable started steering for the distant Rocky Point as *Tulla*'s faithful little Perkins diesel purred away. Amy cleaned up the compact galley after their quick lunch and took over the steering duties.

As he pulled on his raincoat and sou'wester hat, Cable thought about his plan to crab at Rocky Point. *Yes, it could be dangerous, but it could also be very profitable.* Out on deck, he baited up ten pots, shortened the buoy lines to account for the shallower depth at Rocky Point, and stacked them so he could slowly put out a long string of pots by shoving them off the stern of the boat without stopping.

He came inside the cabin and took over the steering, wanting to make a dry run without pots. He explained what he was doing to Amy as he steered toward shore, marking the bottom with the electronic Fathometer. That gave them a good picture of where the pots would go. Then he turned 180 degrees and headed back out. On the next run, they would put out the pots.

When he talked like that, Amy would roll her eyes and give him *the* look. That was one of the reasons she cared for him so much. He was a dreamer, an enthusiast, and an optimist. That was her secret, and she wasn't telling him.

They headed out a bit, took a fix, and turned back in toward the cliff. They were almost there. The waves were crashing against the sheer rock wall so hard they vibrated through the boat. Cable steered *Tulla* in closer.

Amy asked, "How close, Cable?"

"We need to get where the waves hitting the rocks wash out the sand below and make a nice hole for crab dining."

She sighed. "Oh."

Cable reminded her to mind their course since she would be driving on the next pass. The weather was still good, maybe fifteen knots out of the northwest.

Occasionally an eight- to ten-foot swell would come through, rolling with no breakers. "Perfect," he said. "Here we go." He gave Amy the wheel, set the throttle for a steady speed, ran out on deck and started pushing the pots over board, one at a time. *One, one thousand; two one thousand* … He wanted them five big, fat, slow seconds apart. The rock wall was coming closer, so close Amy could see the isolated ferns growing in the crevices. Two pots were still on deck when Amy called out the door, "That's it. We're on the edge of the hole. There's no more water."

"Okay, that's great. Swing around. These last two can go on the ocean side of the hole."

When the last two were dropped off, he went inside, and Amy quickly handed the steering chores back to him.

She went over and sat on the bunk. Her breaths came quickly as she stared at the deck. "Cable Dent, that is just too close for me. Are we going back over to the northwest string now?"

"Yep. You take a nap, pretty girl. It will be an hour of run time. Then we'll start on the uphill side and work our way toward home. That'll be a wrap for the day."

Amy swung her legs up, stretched out on the bunk, and closed her eyes. As he watched her sleep, Cable asked himself why that beautiful woman would want anything to do with a guy like him. Maybe it was time to quit questioning and enjoy what they had.

As they approached the northwest string, he called to Amy to come steer the boat so he could go outside and work the gear. The crabbing was okay, with an average of four to six crabs per pot. The timing was perfect when they reached Port Orford. *Tulla* was next in line under the sling to unload the crab and then slide forward to the hoist to be hauled out.

Jan was running the hoist, and Cable was glad to see his friend. "Hi, Jan."

"How d'you do, you two?"

Amy broke into a smile as she piped up, "Cable is beachcombing for crab now."

Jan laughed, shaking his head. They stepped ashore, and Jan continued to haul *Tulla* the rest of the way up and over to her trailer.

"Same time tomorrow, half hour before daylight, Cable?"

"Yeah, Jan. Bright and early."

Cable picked up their ticket for the day's catch from Mitchell, and they went to the general store, where Amy's folks were waiting dinner for them.

Cable had put in a CB "citizens band" radio base station in the folks' kitchen and one on *Tulla* so they could talk anytime. Amy wanted one put in the shack as well. "Maybe this spring sometime," Cable had said. "We have telephones to take care of that."

Dinner was relaxing. Amy did have to tell her parents about putting gear in the hole in front of Rocky Point.

She said, "If you ever want to watch us work the gear,

stop at Rocky Point on 101, and you'll be standing right above us."

The folks thought that would be interesting.

Amy's dad loved watching the weather. It was such a big part of their lives on the coast. "What do you think we have for weather tomorrow, Dad?" She knew he liked to give them the report every evening.

"Looks like twenty-five miles per hour plus from the northwest out to the reefs. For the coast beach by your Rocky Point string, the wind calms down to ten to fifteen miles per hour. There should be some fog with that. As we all know, it's that time of the year."

"Shouldn't be that bad with the Northwest fifteen," Cable said, "don't you think, Dad?"

"Cable, there isn't much sense going if it's socked in," Amy said.

"Yeah, I know, Amy. I'll go down early. If I can't see the jetty light, we'll wait. I want to get those ten pots out of Rocky Point, or they might sand in on us by the end of next week. Besides, we have the new Decca radar we put in this fall. This would be a good test for it, close in to the rock wall and all."

The conversation drifted away from the weather to Amy's folks' talk about putting in a convenience store with gas and diesel up on Highway 101. This was a longtime dream for Amy's dad.

When the time came to say good night, Cable told Amy he would see her in the early morning, and he walked up the hill to his shack.

CHAPTER 15

At 5:30 a.m., Cable was at the back door knocking quietly to get Amy's attention as she fixed a pot of mush for breakfast. She opened the door quickly. "Come on in. Mush is almost ready." She gave Cable a peck on the cheek and stirred the mush at the same time. Amy laughed, "You'd think we've been together forever."

Amy's dad had it right all along. When they arrived at the hoist, the northwesterly wind was sending swirls of fog around them. "Darn, I can't see the jetty light. Can you, Amy?"

"No, I can't see the store from here either," she said as she stood on the dock by the hoist.

"We'll wait, folks. Maybe by late morning. Darn, I just want to get my pots back."

Amy couldn't help herself. "If you hadn't put the silly things there, you wouldn't be worried about them, would you?"

Cable quickly replied, smiling, "Now that you bring it up, my job is to keep the doors open around here. I just don't want to wear a plastic bow tie up at the folks' 101 gas station."

They all started laughing. Cable was so much like Grandpa Phil, always making jokes about himself.

They waited until 10:30 and had Jan put *Tulla* in the water. Cable didn't bother to fill up the crab live tank. He brought a box to put the crab in on deck. This would need to be a quick trip. Cable figured the fog would close in again by early afternoon.

"Just winter weather, Amy. 'Nothing more, nothing less,' Grandpa would say."

They chugged slowly over to Rocky Point, carefully watching the orange screen on the little twenty-four-mile Decca radar. They also kept a close eye on the Sperry Fathometer, which never failed to tell them the depth of the water.

Cable pulled the boat up in front of Rocky Point. They could see the headlights of a car occasionally peeking through the fog. And every so often as the fog lifted, a clear patch of blue sky and sunlight would shine through.

This would be close. The eight- to ten-foot swells rolled in and smashed against the steep rock cliff, with the back swells ricocheting back out to sea and hitting *Tulla*. "Guess there could be better days, Amy, my pretty girl."

"Let's get in there and get it done, so we can get out of here," Amy said, her lips tight with worry.

"All right. We'll swing in. I'll grab a buoy and hand it to the pot hauler as you swing around to stem the swells. Just put the swells right on our nose, please."

"Will we save those two outer pots for last?"

"Yes. And remember, don't make any sharp turns. We don't want to get a line in the propeller, right?"

"Right, Captain."

"If the fog socks in, head west for our bailout. Holler through the door to me if anything at all doesn't look right to you, please."

"You can be sure of that, Mr. Fisherman."

Out on deck, Cable was comfortable with what they were doing. Amy was a hell of a girl to have the grit to get in there and do this job.

On the first pass, once out of the hole, she slowed down while Cable had the hydraulics screaming to haul the first pot up as fast as he could.

Cable hollered into Amy, "Feels like a heavy one, pretty girl. Come on, everyone, we're having crab for dinner tonight!" When the pot was alongside the boat, he saw it was full, with another four big, fat crabs lying on top of the pot.

Cable dropped to his knees, leaned out over the side, and flipped the crab on board before they could crawl off the top of the pot. He placed the pot on the sorting table and put the keepers in the boxes on deck.

"The weather's coming up," Cable said as he took a quick look around. "I'll fill the live tank in the fish hold to make her ride better with some weight in her tummy."

"Good idea. You want me to start the next pass?"

"Go ahead and start your swing. I'll be ready for the next one." Amy steered carefully, swinging *Tulla* around to pick up the second and third pots.

On the fourth pot, Cable could occasionally make out the rock cliff. He hooked the pot and looked up at the cliff when he heard the screeching of brakes and tires screaming out frantically, trying to grip the road.

Tulla was only forty feet out from the rock cliff. Cable was thinking whatever was making all that noise was headed straight for them. Next came the crushing sound of metal against metal and hard rock. The first thought to cross his mind was of the guardrails above them were being torn out.

"Amy, full throttle, now! Head west!" Cable yelled. She couldn't hear the crashing sounds with the engine running, but she didn't hesitate when she caught the urgency in Cable's voice. She slammed the throttle to the dash and steered out to sea.

Cable looked up again. First, he saw the headlights and then the flat front end of a yellow school bus. Everything was happening in slow motion. He watched as the front end of the bus slowly slid over the edge of the cliff. But it didn't stop. It just kept coming.

Tipping ever so slowly, the old yellow bus went nose down, headed for a twenty-foot outcrop. He saw the bus slam into the rocks, the front-end crumpling with the impact. Just then, the fog closed in tightly, and he couldn't see the headlights anymore.

Amy yelled, "What was that?"

"Slow down to an idle. I need to bring the pot in."

Amy was standing at the cabin back door. "Cable?"

"You won't believe this. I wouldn't either if I hadn't seen it. An old school bus drove over the cliff. Listen close. You can hear people screaming over the hydraulics. We need to go back in and help those people, if the bus hasn't slid off the lower shelf yet."

Stopping the pot hauler, Cable pulled the pot on board; emptied it; and threw the pot, buoy line and all, onto the stern end of the boat. "I'll drive from outside Amy, you stand by the mast and watch for me. We'll nose into the rock cliff. *Tulla* is a double-ender, so she can back out straight into the seas if she needs to."

Concentrating on managing the boat against the sea swells, he eased in toward the rock wall. Amy yelled, "There, right there." She pointed toward the cliff. "I see the top of the bus. It's just hanging on the edge waiting to go into the ocean."

Cable pulled in as careful as he could. "Amy, call your folks on the CB, have them phone the state patrol and the coast guard. Make a call out to any boats in our area and tell them we need help."

"What are you going to do, Cable?"

"We'll run out, put out our anchor, back down as far as it's safe, and then put out a stern anchor. We'll use the inflatable life raft so I can paddle back to them."

"You could go up on the rocks with the raft."

"No. You'll have a crab line on me and can pull me back with the crab block. We'll be fine. Now make the calls, will you? I'll get us set up."

They were a good team. They both did exactly as Cable had explained. *Tulla* stemmed the growing swells with her bow, set the bow anchor, and then backed down toward the rock cliff face slacking out the anchor line at the same time.

Tulla's stern anchor fetched up just right as well, close enough that they could make out the bus perched on the shelf of the cliff, like it belonged there. They could still hear the screams and cries for help from the people inside the bus. Amy's heart ached for them.

Quickly getting the inflatable raft off the top of *Tulla*'s house, Cable put it on deck and slid it over the side as he pulled the lanyard. The raft immediately inflated, riding right side up on the swells, which were up to ten feet now.

The swells were smooth, and nothing was breaking on top. *This is okay*, Cable thought, *just a nice ten-foot-long roller*. *Tulla* rode easy over the tops of the swells.

Cable grabbed a single-sheave block that could unlatch at the cheek—a snatch block. His plan was to tie the pulley to the bus and run a bite of the crab pot buoy line through it. Then Amy could pull the raft to and from the bus with the crab block.

"Once I have a load of people in the raft, you can pull the raft back to *Tulla*. Easy huh?" As Amy listened to his plan, she was still scared and not sure this would all work. But she trusted Cable with her life, and she knew that, if anyone could do this, it would be Cable.

"What about signals?" she asked.

"I'll take the handheld light. So three shorts means stop; two longs means pull; and arms waving like crazy means stop, stop, stop."

Amy said, "With this swell, I can only see you half the time. What about the fog, Cable? It could come back in."

"We'll be okay. Let's get going. Did you have Mom get a hold of Jan at the hoist, so he could call more boats?"

"Yes."

"He might get John to put in his new boat and help us. I'll have to paddle in the first time. Don't let anyone come alongside unless they have big airbag fenders. They could damage us and sink *Tulla*."

Amy nodded. Her face was full of worry and fear. Cable put on a lifejacket and crawled over the side into the little raft as it banged against the side of Tulla. He checked that the pulley was there and well tied. "Okay, slack me out, pretty girl."

CHAPTER 16

Amy blew him a kiss and started slacking off. Cable had a hard time paddling with the fish-hold bend-board he'd grabbed for a temporary paddle. Now swells came up that catapulted him closer to shore and shot him down the front side of the swell like a roller coaster without tracks.

This isn't so bad.

As he reached the front of the bus, he could see the reader board above the windshield. It read "The Church of Our Faith." That made Cable wonder who was in the bus. Faith of what? That didn't make any sense.

He quickly flashed the light three shorts, and Amy stopped him on a dime in front of the bus passenger door. As the door folded open, a man with graying hair stood above the steps. He was about Cable's size and thirty years older, Cable guessed.

Cable needed to grab the rearview mirror by the door. He reached for it at the top of the swell, but just couldn't quite grab it. He could see the folks trapped inside the bus watching him. On the fourth try, he finally got a line over the mirror, tied his block to it, and took some slack out of the crab line.

The ashen face of the man in the doorway told Cable how scared he was.

"Hi," Cable said. "You ready to get out of here?" As the swells rolled through, Cable and the raft would rise and fall eight to ten feet and then the back swell would ricochet off the rock wall and hit him again. *The swells are long. That gives me some time between them.*

The man in the doorway grabbed both sides of the stair railing and said, "No. We saw you coming and decided to wait for help from above on the highway."

Cable couldn't believe he'd heard right. Working to keep his balance in the raft, he said, "We put in a call for help. I'm sure they'll be right along. So, what you're telling me is you don't want my help?"

By now, most of the passenger's windows were open, and Cable could see the many scared faces staring out at him. "Let me help you here." Cable started to explain calmly. "You have the top of the swell lapping up against your bumper right now, and we're at the bottom of the tide …"

"No, we'll wait. Thank you," the man said, not giving Cable a chance to finish.

"Okay now," Cable started again. "Let's slow down and think for a minute. We have a seven-foot tide today. In six hours, the water will be where you're standing. That's not the problem. The problem is the swells that come with it and the power of all that water. That's—"

The man cut Cable off again. "I told you we'll wait. It's been decided. We will pray, brothers and sisters."

"Mister, all the praying in the world ain't going to stop that tide, and for darn sure it ain't stopping the power of the ocean. You think real hard, 'cuz that could rip the front end of this bus right off its perch. Then it will slip into the twenty-foot hole in the water in front of you and lay on its side."

The man's face went from ashen gray to pasty white. He didn't say a word as Cable bobbed up and down, riding the swells in front of him.

The other passengers started yelling. They had heard everything Cable had said, and they wanted out. "Brother, you can't decide for all of us. You're just driving the bus, and you put us here in the first place!" The crowd started to stand up, but no one dared move. They believed Cable was right.

"Now, Brothers and Sisters, the Lord will watch out for us," the pasty-faced man said.

Cable wanted to help. "Mister, if he was watching out for everyone, you wouldn't be down here staring at a watery grave. So, what's it going to be?"

"We wait. It's God's divine hand that put us here. It is God's hand that will help us," he quickly replied.

"Yeah," Cable said. "I'm here to help. This could be God's divine hand. Don't you see help is here? Just give me your children. They have a long life to live," Cable yelled, losing his patience as he continued to bob up and down. The swells were getting madder by the minute.

He looked up toward the cliff and couldn't see to the

top, so rescuers would have a problem seeing the bus now that the fog had settled in. Just then, an eerie white veil closed around everything, and he couldn't see Amy and *Tulla* either.

He could tell she had shut down the engine and was listening. He yelled, "Amy? Amy, are you there? Can you hear me?"

"Yes, Cable. I'm here."

"This jackass doesn't want to go. He would rather the Lord help them than you and me."

Cable knew what he was doing. He had to put a fire under those who didn't want to fall on a self-righteous sword. Cable thanked Grandpa for teaching him how to do that.

A middle-aged man came down to the front of the bus. "Hell no! Let us out of here!" He picked up the gray-haired man and threw him over to the driver's seat.

Pointing his finger at the driver, he said, "Sit. And shut up. You're fired."

He smiled at Cable. "Could you take me and my family out to your boat?"

"Sure. That's why I'm here. Now the way I see it working, you need to pass me a person when I come up to the top of the swell. Got it?"

"How many can you take?" asked the man.

"Five in the boat. We can put more in the water with life jackets on," answered Cable.

"Okay. Five in the boat and two in the water. Let's do it." He was ready.

"First, pass me your wife or any adult and then give

me the children, and the old folks come last." Amy had thrown three spare lifejackets into the raft just as Cable had gotten in. "It's cold in the water," he warned. "Whoever goes in needs to know that."

"Okay, I'll send my four kids and parents. My wife and someone can go into the water. I'll stay."

"No. I need you at the boat to help Amy."

"All right. Let's do it."

Cable was already soaked and shivering. His teeth chattered.

First came Granny. *This isn't old folks last, but let's just get 'em in the raft,* Cable thought. He was glad to start the rescue, as no other help had arrived yet. When the raft was at the top of the swell, Granny stepped over to Cable, holding both hands out. Cable caught her wrists, jerked her into the life raft, and gently threw her forward in a heap.

At the top of the next swell, Grandpa had one hand out, and his son held the other hand. When Cable took hold, Grandpa jumped into Cable's arms and went to his knees, dragging Cable down with him.

"Go forward. Children come next. You tend to them." Two swells later, the four-year-old was scared but brave. His dad handed him to Cable. Cable snatched the boy and handed him to Grandpa and Grandma. Three more kids went in the raft, ages up to fifteen, almost the same age as Cable. *I'll be darned,* he thought.

"The wife and sister come next. After you put life jackets on, come over to me and I'll tie a line around you, and then you'll slip into the water, okay?"

They gave a scared nod.

Cable handed them the life jackets. They slipped into the water and started shaking immediately from the cold. Cable tied a line around the father, and into the water he went. He wrapped his arms around the two ladies and hung onto the stern of the raft.

There was an eerie quiet except for the swells breaking on the rocks. Cable yelled as loudly as he could, "Okay, Amy. Reel us in." He heard the little diesel start up and the screeching of the hydraulics. They started to move.

Not even a minute later, they were alongside *Tulla*, sitting under her crab block. There was Amy with a big smile. "It's about time."

"Grandpa, you first and then help the others." He was a spry old man and sprang up and over the rail. They took the four children off the boat. "Grandma, you stay. I need your weight in the bow. Okay ladies, you're next." Cable practically ripped them out of the water as Amy and Grandpa helped them onto the deck of *Tulla*.

"I need those lifejackets, ladies. Now you, Dad." Cable was still on his knees in the stern of the life raft. He grabbed the father by the lifejacket and hauled him over the stern like a two hundred-pound fish. They lay in the bottom of the raft for a split second. Cable smiled. "Help Mom off. And then you, okay? I want you to stay and help Amy. She's in charge on the boat."

The man nodded, and Amy smiled. "Got more boats coming. Jan has a CB radio in his truck. He got a hold of John, and he should be in the water by now."

"Okay. Big airbag fenders and no damage to *Tulla,* right?"

"Yes, Captain. No damage."

The fog was settling in thick, and they couldn't see the bus from the boat. "You're so cold, Cable." Amy saw him starting to shake, and his jaw was moving rapidly. "Get me back there. I'll yell when to stop me. If you need to, shut off the engine and slack me back. The dad will help you. Okay, love you, pretty girl."

Chapter 17

"All right. Let's do it."

And back Cable went.

The tide was coming in at a faster rate. When the swell rushed by, it lapped at the bottom of the bus door. Coming to a stop, Cable hollered, "Any takers?"

Another strong-looking, younger dad was standing in the door. "We're ready. Tell me what you want us to do."

Cable was on his knees in an inch of icy cold water in the bottom of the raft. "Good. One adult first and then bring me the kids. Here are the jackets for the ones who go into the water. As each swell comes up, have one ready for me. We need to move fast. The tide's coming in. What's your name?"

"Bob."

"Okay, Bob. You stay to help. My name is Cable."

Bob chuckled at that.

"Yeah, I know. My Grandpa had a sense of humor. I'll tell you about it later."

They loaded two older folks, four kids, and three in the water, just like the last time.

"Amy, pull away," he yelled. The little Perkins started

up with the familiar squeal of the crab block hydraulics, and then Cable felt the raft of scared people move off into the fog.

Alongside *Tulla*, they unloaded the life raft first, and then the people were pulled out of the water.

"Amy, where is John? Is he the only help we have?"

"Yes, he's trying to find us now. I don't want to load *Tulla* anymore until we unload some."

"Have them sit back aft on the stern. Keep her trim. No mistakes. Give me the jackets. Let's go."

Amy could see Cable was having problems using his hands because of the cold. "Slack me back. You have to stop me before I go on the rocks, okay?"

"Okay, Cable," Amy said. She was very worried about Cable, but she knew he wouldn't stop until everyone was off the bus.

The life raft and Cable disappeared into the fog for the next load. The same as before, there were three in the water and four forward in the raft with Cable. As he called to Amy, she yelled back that John had finally arrived. As the raft pulled up to *Tulla*, John's new boat was tied off, and he was already loading people onto it. He hopped over the rail onto *Tulla*, next to Amy. Cable said, "John, thanks for coming."

"You just can't stay away from helping people, can you?"

"We have old Phil to thank for that." Cable groaned. They all three laughed. It was good to break the stress.

As they moved people off the raft, Cable said to John, "Take these three groups to the hoist and then come back, okay? That's just in case something goes haywire on us and to get any overflow of people." Cable turned to the dad. "How many are in the bus?"

The dad was standing by Amy and John. "I think we had forty."

"All right. Jackets, Amy. Let's go get some more."

The rhythm of the swells was their saving grace, Cable thought.

The next load was number four, and he took nine more people to *Tulla*. That left five on the bus for the last load. The water was now up to two feet in the bus door when the swells crested.

Cable got into the raft and said, "Amy, love, this is it. Five to go."

She could see his lips were blue and not working very well when he tried to talk, making him hard to understand.

As Cable approached the bus for the last load, he heard a distant shout. "Hello on the bus!" He had to stop and look around. He looked up the cliff beyond the back of the bus and saw two rescue workers repelling down the cliff. The closest one shouted something, but Cable couldn't hear him above the ocean's roar against the rock cliff. The rescuer came further down the cliff wall to the rear bumper of the bus. "How many more before everyone is out of the bus?"

Cable cupped his hands around his mouth and shouted, "This is the last trip. Then she's all yours."

"All right. We'll hook the wrecker to it and wait up top for you to finish taking them off."

As the workers hooked up the towline, Cable shouted,

"You be careful. The tide's coming in fast, and the bus could slip off the ledge anytime."

One worker waved and said, "We'll get clear as soon as we can."

Cable turned his attention to the remaining passengers. They all transferred to the raft, even Bob, and he had done a hell of a job passing over people.

The last person left was the pasty-faced, gray-haired driver, the divine hand believer.

"Come on. Let's go now," Cable said, holding his hand out.

The driver was standing in freezing water up to his waist. He said, "No, it's God's will that I stay."

Cable was out of patience. "Well, okay. Let's shake hands, and I can wish you luck." He reached out to the man. As the man gave his hand for a shake, Cable grabbed it and squeezed hard as a vice and jerked him into the bottom of the raft into his arms.

Cable looked him in the eye, smiled, and quietly said, "You've been saved by the divine hand of Cable Dent."

Quickly reaching over to the bus mirror, he cut the line holding his snatch block, threw it in the raft, and hollered, "Okay, Amy. Haul us in, please."

Tulla's little diesel started up, and the hydraulics came on, squealing as the raft with the last of the people started to move for the last time. "Thank God," Cable said under his breath.

With no one in the water this time, the little raft moved easier. They came alongside *Tulla* and unloaded swiftly. Cable came aboard, stiff from the cold and having trouble moving around as he tied off the raft.

"Everyone, please sit down. I know you want to see. This is a little boat, and you need to keep spread out. And please sit down!" Cable looked at the divine hand guy with the gray hair. "That means you. Sit down."

The man nodded and sat down on the hatch cover.

Cable had Amy shift the hydraulics from the crab block to the anchor winch located behind the mast. He pulled the stern anchor first, getting it in the clear and on board in minutes. Taking three turns of line, he turned on the hydraulics again, and the bow anchor line started to come in. Then it stopped. "Amy, I need you to stand by the wheel."

Hauling the anchor rope until the chain came aboard, Cable could tell the bow anchor was fouled. *Probably with old crab pot lines.* "Don't put her in gear until I clear the anchor, Amy. It could get in the wheel."

"Okay, Cable. How do I know when we're clear?"

"The anchor will come on board easily."

Cable crawled forward on his knees and lay on his belly as he looked over the bow. The swells were bigger and deeper now, building with the flood tide and the wind freshening. "Open your window, Amy, so I can talk to you."

Sure enough, there was old pot line wrapped around the anchor. Cable had his 14-inch bait knife with him and tried to pull it out. His hands were so cold he could hardly feel the knife handle. He reached over the side but couldn't reach the line because his life jacket was getting in the way.

He pressed down on his belly even more and hung out over the bow. He held onto the stanchion with one hand and cut the pot line off with the other. The line was old and hard and wrapped tightly around the anchor. Cutting as quickly as he could, he knew that *Tulla* and all on board could be smashed up on the rocks in the next two swells if he couldn't get the line cut.

Finally, the knife cut through and their anchor was cleared. He rolled up on his side and called, "Okay, Amy. We're clear. Get us out of here."

Amy put *Tulla* in gear, closed the wheelhouse window, and gave her some throttle at the same time they were quartering the seas. Taking the crest of the swell on the port bow, *Tulla* dipped, and the wave washed the bow clean, including Cable.

When the foam and water cleared, Amy screamed, "He's gone! Cable's overboard!"

She slowed *Tulla*, screaming, "Everyone, look for Cable!" They all rushed to the starboard side and, doing so, laid *Tulla* over on her side to a dangerous point.

Amy's helper yelled as Amy fought to control the boat. "Everyone, sit down and spread out!" As folks pulled their way back to the seats, *Tulla* righted herself and made it through the next two huge swells. But Cable was gone.

Amy screamed again, "Let go of the raft, he might see it. I'll call for help. Bob, go back and cut the line to the raft." Amy slowed *Tulla* even more to listen for Cable calling her for help, but there were no calls for help. Cable was gone, just like that.

"You need to take the people in. The boat is not stable," Bob said to Amy.

She had tears streaming down her cheeks and nodded her head at the same time.

What they did hear was the final crashing and grinding of steel on the sliver of rock beach at the bottom of the cliff. The bus was gone. It would have taken the wreckers with it if an alert operator hadn't released the winch brake to let the bus fall. The sea had washed out the ledge under the front of the bus, just like Cable had told them it would. Everyone on the boat got quiet, thinking of how lucky they were to have been rescued by this young man and woman with their little boat.

Amy turned *Tulla* and chugged away toward the hoist.

CHAPTER 18

Cable rolled over in the life jacket and his face came out of the water. He could hear *Tulla* pulling away and a frantic scream from Amy. "Cut the raft loose. Cut it loose now!"

Cable couldn't see *Tulla*, but he could hear her. He tried to swim towards her engine noise. Then she was gone. Now he was in a shroud of fog and freezing cold. He pulled himself into a tight ball to try to keep some warmth.

Looking up, he saw the life raft bobbing and floating by on a swell. It was no more than twenty feet away, but it might as well have been two miles. Cable mustered every frozen ounce of strength he had to dog paddle toward the raft. As he stretched out his hand, the raft went by him, pushed by the swell. He just missed it. "No, God!" he cried. *I need to make it for my family and Grandpa's memory.*

Out of the corner of his eye, he saw the bowline snaking through the water behind the raft. Six strong strokes of his arms pulled him to the line. He put his half-frozen arm over the line and then kept turning his arm in a circle to wrap the bowline around it. *If I'm going to die, I want them to have a body to bury next to my family on the hill.*

He hung on with the last bit of strength he had. The raft came to a halt. Cable floated in the water, panting, cramps starting in his arms and then his legs. He had reached his limit. He tried to relax his muscles. The life jacket was holding him up and he could breathe easily, not fighting to keep water out of his face.

Ever so slowly, Cable pulled on the line and the raft came closer. That took forever. And then the little raft bumped him in the head. What a wonderful feeling to have it nudge him so softly, while the swells were building even more.

Cable knew this was not the end of his struggle. He still needed to ride the raft to the sandy beach where Amy had first kissed him. *Wouldn't you know it? It had to end where it started.* Cable wasn't thinking too clearly now, but he was still thinking.

Buried in the fog, Cable guessed he was drifting north to the fatal shore. He remembered the raft's boarding rope ladder, and forced his arms to reach up for the ladder that was built into the raft. He pulled down, and the rope ladder dropped out of its pouch. *Thank you God for the small things that make life possible.*

So far so good, he thought to himself. *Let's see if I can get in there. If I wait too long, I won't have any strength left.* He pulled his feet up and worked off both fishing boots. He shoved a foot in the rope ladder rung and pulled on the handles on the side of the raft. Giving a push with the other foot, he came half out of the water and lay over the side of the raft. As he rolled to his side and fell into the bottom of the raft, he felt four inches of water lapping against his face.

He lay there panting and staring up at the dark gray sky. A cold, damp fog drifted over him through the dim light. Evening was here. *It ain't gonna get better.*

Thank you, God, again. Don't know what I'd do without ya. Now if I don't crash into some rocks, I think I have a chance. Untangling his foot from the ladder, he curled up in a ball to save whatever warmth he could preserve and hopefully regain some of that precious energy he'd chewed up earlier.

He lay there for a long while, passing in and out of consciousness. Then he remembered there was a first aid kit on board with an aluminum blanket in it. Maybe he could wrap himself up and keep some heat in. The sound of crashing waves on the rocks was fading away. *All right, we're drifting north with the current. Now we have a chance, little raft.* He thought that, with a little luck, he might land on the long, sandy beach just below Port Orford where he and Amy had shared their first kiss. *The store is only a mile up the beach. I could sure use some warm cocoa and the girl of my dreams.*

Cable managed to get the aluminum blanket out and wrapped around him. Curled up in the bottom of the raft, he worked hard to scrape up every bit of energy he could. The pounding of the surf was steadily getting louder and louder. *I'm getting closer to the beach.* He guessed there was only about twenty feet of visibility. *Okay, raft, we're going to the end together.*

He felt the rise of the swells getting bigger under him. That meant they were getting closer with each big roller. As the little raft approached the beach, the surge kept getting faster. At the top of the swell, it started to break, making a hissing sound in the dark.

Let's time this out. I can feel the sets—one, two, three. This is the big one. Now three more, and we should be there. On the third swell, the raft started sliding down the face of the swell and then slammed on the sandy bottom as the backside of the swell came crashing down on him with the sound of a locomotive, almost turning the raft over.

We've landed. It's just you and me, little buddy.

Cable was so cold and stiff he could barely move his limbs. They were frozen. With great effort, he got up on his knees just as the next swell slammed down, forcing his face into the bottom of the raft and flattening him out again. This one washed the raft farther up the beach and filled it with water. Now the raft couldn't move.

He forced himself up to his knees again. It was pitch-black out, and he had no idea which way the beach was. The next wave hit him square in the back. *Okay, thank you for that, Phil. The beach is straight ahead,* Cable told himself. *Yes, Grandpa. I knew you would be here.*

He crawled out of the raft on all fours and clawed his way farther away from the pounding surf. *Thank you, God and Grandpa and whoever else was here for me, because I know I didn't do this on my own.*

Once out of reach of the surf, Cable curled back into a ball and waited to collect up what little strength he had left to make it home to Amy, the future Mrs. Dent.

CHAPTER 19

Amy had to run *Tulla* back over to the hoist, and she had never run the boat totally alone. John found her on radar and talked her into where he was. When he first pulled up within earshot, Amy came out on deck with tears streaming down her face. "John, we need to go back to look for Cable."

John came alongside *Tulla* and took more people onto his boat.

"Amy, let's get unloaded and hauled. Cable will be headed for the beach right now, as we speak. I know this place. He's safe. Believe me. Trust me. I know your man and the tide. If he didn't make the beach, then he didn't make it, and he won't make it. You can't see nothing out there with the fog and the dark closing in. Let's take care of these people right now."

Amy asked Bob to help her rig the slings to haul *Tulla*. She was under the forward hoist, and John took the back hoist. They hooked the gear, and Jan took out the slack, like he had done so many times before.

Hauling her up to ground level, Jan stopped at the wall so all the rescued people could climb out onto the boatyard. The yard was crowded as emergency personnel started rendering assistance to the frightened and half-frozen people from the bus.

Amy's mom and dad were there at the rail with open arms for her. Mother asked, "Where's Cable? What, what happened to our Cable?"

Amy's eyes were red from crying so much. "He's gone, Mom. He washed overboard when he was getting the anchor cleared. He's still out there. We let go of the raft. We can only hope and pray he caught it and climbed in."

Jan came over. "Amy, I'll take care of *Tulla*. You go on home with your parents."

"No, Jan. I'm not leaving. My guy is out there, and I want to go get him, whatever the price."

John Dill caught up with Amy and her folks. "Hey, I thought we would go look. He isn't gone yet, ya know. Amy, I told you he'll be fine. He's just waiting for a ride to your shack. Now, let's go get him."

John hollered for everyone to get into his power wagon. "The old four-wheel-drive will get us down to the beach," he said. "I think he's down there, waiting for a ride. Alisha, you, Amy, and Mrs. Berquist get in the front with me."

Amy's dad, Jan, Mitchell, and two others jumped into the back. John handed them a spotlight, running the cord out his window to power it.

At the beach road, John dropped the truck down to low range and put it in four-wheel-drive. "When we find him, I have a couple of blankets we can wrap him in.

They're stored in back of the seat." John smiled, praying that Cable had made it to the beach.

He counted on finding Cable. That was all there was to it. He drove very slowly down the foggy beach with the spotlight from the back and the truck's headlights shining a bright path for them. They drove closer to the waterline.

Amy saw something and cried out, "Look! What's that?"

John hit the brakes and then drove slowly toward the lump in the surf. It was hard to make anything out with the darkness and heavy mist of the fog. Amy flew out the passenger door before John could get the truck stopped. Everyone else piled out of the back. Amy ran to the lump, turned, and yelled, "It's the raft. I don't see any foot prints."

John yelled back over the roar of the surf, "Okay, let's get down the beach. I know he's here. Things don't go more than another two hundred yards down the beach.

Driving slowly another couple hundred yards along the tide line, they came to another lump. They stopped short of the lump so the headlights shined on it. Cable heard Amy calling and rolled over on his back. Amy ran to him and threw herself on him.

"Oh, Cable," she said, crying with relief, "I wasn't sure if I would ever see you again." Turning to everyone, Amy sobbed, "Thank you. Thank you, everyone."

Cable was too cold to talk.

John helped get Cable up and wrapped his two blankets around him. He had known Cable would be there. The tide always brought the drift there. He'd learned that when he was beachcombing as a kid.

With everyone standing around being thankful Cable was alive, John said, "Okay, let's take him home."

They put Cable in the back of the power wagon, and Amy held his head. John started back to the emergency folks who were still at the hoist.

Cable managed to get a few words out. "Amy, I just want to go to the shack."

"Yes, Cable."

"Is *Tulla* locked up? We still have crab in the tank."

Amy smiled, tears of happiness on her cheeks, "Cable, sometimes … Mitchell took care of that. And I pumped out the live tank before Jan hauled us. I knew you would ask about that."

"We have a lot of fish to catch next summer, you know," Cable said weakly.

As they pulled into the boatyard, an emergency person came to the truck to checked Cable over. He said he was a little worse for the wear but could go home. John drove everyone up to the shack.

Cable tried walking but needed help. "Think my legs are a little cold."

Jan and Amy's dad helped get him into the shack and bedroom.

Amy stood him up in the center of the bedroom and undressed and redressed him in dry long johns while her dad held him up.

They helped Cable to the couch while Jan lit the stove, and Mother fixed hot drinks for all. Cable huddled up with Amy, who sat close by his side. Everyone was happy to be in the old shack having coffee and warming up. Someone remarked that they were sure old Phil had helped that night. Cable was sure both God and Grandpa had been there in the raft with him.

***

The next morning, Cable woke up covered in the heavy blankets Amy had spread over him. He climbed out of bed, feeling "stiffer than a plank" as Grandpa would say. The shack was still warm, but not that warm. He went to the stove, turned up the heat, and sat at the table in his long johns, trying to wake up.

He thought about all that had happened the previous day. Looking up at the sound of the back door opening, he saw Amy coming through the door with a big smile. She wrapped her arms around his shoulders.

"How's my beautiful girl today?" Cable said as he took her hand and pulled her around to his lap. "Thank you for everything yesterday. Thanks for helping with all the people and for sticking with me. I want to go into town today and buy a ring set. You pick careful now. It'll have to last you a lifetime."

She stood up and faced him. "What happened out there?"

"You promise you won't laugh at me?"

"No, I never laugh at you. Well, maybe with you when you're joking, and that's quite often."

Cable got serious. "Grandpa, he was there in my mind. Anyway, he had some suggestions. Maybe it was the scrape with death. I would have died if you hadn't cut the life raft loose. Grandpa told me I needed to make us a couple forever, being that you saved me.

"Hold on. That's not coming out right. Anyway, Amy, I want to marry you and share my life with you. I know I'm young, but I'm good for it—a lifetime, that is. We can even throw in a couple of rug rats built by you and me. No big hurry on that part, mind you now."

"Oh, Cable! Are you crazy?"

"No, I just want to be with you, no one else."

"Okay, my fisherman. You got a deal. Now, can I fish the season with you next year?"

"I'm not going without my partner."

"I can't believe it! We need to take this slow!"

"Okay. I just want you to know what I have on my mind. First, I want to sit down with the folks. I'm going to make them an offer, a partnership, for your dad's convenience store dream up on 101. Be sure to bring the checkbook.

"This will be a partnership between their family and our family. They're good people. I trust them. After next season, we'll make plans to build a new house where the shack is. You should be okay with that."

"Why? Why all the changes, Cable? What happened to you out there?"

"I don't know for sure, but I almost lost everything, and that's brought me closer to what I want in life. And that's you. I heard someplace that you would complete my circle."

She leaned across the table, kissing him on the lips, and saying yes to a long, happy life of being together.

"Cable, sometimes …"

EPILOGUE

Cable and Amy eventually married. They even built a house where the shack was and finished school to boot. Amy went on to college and earned a degree in accounting.

Cable fished every summer with Amy as his partner and went to college during the winter to keep her company, ending up with a teaching degree. As soon as their children could walk, they took them fishing with them.

"Grandpa, you raised me right with the *Tulla*. Now Amy and I are raising our children right on the *Tulla II*. Thank you, Grandpa, wherever you are."

GLOSSARY

bailout. The captain always has a plan to get the boat out of trouble if whatever he or she is doing goes wrong.

beachcomb. To drive the boat along the shoreline, just barely offshore

blue water (62° Fahrenheit) vs. colder, green water. Tuna live in blue water, dart into the cold green water to feed, and then return to the warmer, blue water.

cheek. The side of the sheave; see **snatch block**.

cockpit. Where the boat steering is, usually an open well in the deck of a boat outside the cabin.

cockpit coaming. A raised edge, as around the cockpit or a hatchway, to keep water out.

combined seas. The combined height of wind wave and sea swell.

cotton out of her seams. Wooden boats have cotton roving pounded in between the wood, which is then tarred to make it water tight. Very rough seas can loosen the cotton causing water to enter the boat.

crab block. A heavy-duty pulley specifically designed for a crab pot line.

equinox. The day, twice a year, when the sun is perpendicular to the earth, causing day and night to be exactly twelve hours. Once the equinox passes, the sea currents change. North of the equator, the Pacific Ocean current flows southerly after the spring equinox and northerly after the autumn equinox.

feather jigs. A gang of hooks weighted with metal and dressed with hair, feathers, and so on.

fetched up. To "set" the anchor, bury it in sand, or hook on rocks.

fish station. Where fishing boats unload their catch and weigh it.

fix. The position of the boat recorded in longitude/latitude or bearing. (1)

flood tide. The incoming tide.

following sea. Waves and swells running in the same direction as the boat, usually running faster than the boat, pushing the boat along. Sometimes not a pleasant ride.

foredeck. Forward part of the main deck, in front of the cabin.

gear out. To lower the trolling poles with lines and jigs into the water.

green waterline. Where coastal water, typically fifty nautical miles offshore, changes to open ocean water, referred to as blue water.

gunwales. The upper edge of the side of a boat, above the deck extending to a cap rail.

heave-to. Adjusting the speed of the boat to make little headway, either in a storm or to stay in the current position.

jigs. A hook attached to a lead sinker, usually covered by some type of bait used to attract fish. Jigs are formed to create a jerky, vertical motion.

jetty. A breakwater constructed of huge granite stones to protect or defend a harbor, stretch of coast, or riverbank.

knots. Speed measured in nautical miles per hour.

loran. Electronic navigation system that shows the boat's current position in longitude and latitude.

port. The left side of the boat looking toward the bow.

quarter the sea. To aim the boat's bow at a forty-five-degree angle to oncoming waves.

sea buoy. A navigation aid anchored well out at sea, usually marking the approach to a river bar or harbor.

sea-kindly. Said of a boat that can handle rough weather; such a boat is also referred to as *seaworthy*.

single sheave block. A sheave is a pulley with a grooved wheel for holding a rope. The grooved wheel spins inside the frame of the sheave. The words sheave and pulley are sometimes used interchangeably. A single sheave uses only one pulley. (3)

snatch block. A block with a hinged side that can be opened to allow a bight of line to be looped over the sheave.

stabilizer. Long poles with vanes attached that can be lowered into the water to reduce side-to-side boat roll.

starboard. The right side of the boat looking toward the bow.

stem the swells. To point the boat directly into the swell.

trolling poles. Long poles attached to the side of the boat that can be raised and lowered. Each pole has a number of baited lines that trail in the water.

wave surge. When large waves push the water much higher than sea level.

wind freshening. Said to mean that wind is starting to increase

Sources

(1) Discoverboating.com/resources/glossary
(2) seatalk.info/cgi-bin/nautical-marine-sailing-
     dictionary
(3) Wikipedia.org
(4) Dictionary.com